Elizabeth Ferrars and The Murder Room

>>> This title is part of The Murder Room, our series dedicated to making available out-of-print or hard-to-find titles by classic crime writers.

Crime fiction has always held up a mirror to society. The Victorians were fascinated by sensational murder and the emerging science of detection; now we are obsessed with the forensic detail of violent death. And no other genre has so captivated and enthralled readers.

Vast troves of classic crime writing have for a long time been unavailable to all but the most dedicated frequenters of second-hand bookshops. The advent of digital publishing means that we are now able to bring you the backlists of a huge range of titles by classic and contemporary crime writers, some of which have been out of print for decades.

From the genteel amateur private eyes of the Golden Age and the femmes fatales of pulp fiction, to the morally ambiguous hard-boiled detectives of mid twentieth-century America and their descendants who walk our twenty-first century streets, The Murder Room has it all. **>>>**

The Murder Room
Where Criminal Minds Meet

themurderroom.com

Elizabeth Ferrars (1907–1995)

One of the most distinguished crime writers of her generation, Elizabeth Ferrars was born Morna Doris MacTaggart in Rangoon and came to Britain at the age of six. She was a pupil at Bedales school between 1918 and 1924, studied journalism at London University and published her first crime novel, *Give a Corpse a Bad Name*, in 1940, the year that she met her second husband, academic Robert Brown. Highly praised by critics, her brand of intelligent, gripping mysteries was also beloved by readers. She wrote over seventy novels and was also published (as E. X. Ferrars) in the States, where she was equally popular. *Ellery Queen Mystery Magazine* described her as 'the writer who may be the closest of all to Christie in style, plotting and general milieu', and the *Washington Post* called her 'a consummate professional in clever plotting, characterization and atmosphere'. She was a founding member of the Crime Writers Association, who, in the early 1980s, gave her a lifetime achievement award.

By Elizabeth Ferrars
(published in The Murder Room)

Toby Dyke
Murder of a Suicide (1941)
 aka *Death in Botanist's Bay*

Police Chief Raposo
Skeleton Staff (1969)
Witness Before the Fact (1979)

Superintendent Ditteridge
A Stranger and Afraid (1971)
Breath of Suspicion (1972)
Alive and Dead (1974)

Virginia Freer
Last Will and Testament (1978)
Frog in the Throat (1980)
I Met Murder (1985)
Beware of the Dog (1992)

Andrew Basnett
The Crime and the Crystal (1985)
The Other Devil's Name (1986)
A Murder Too Many (1988)
A Hobby of Murder (1994)
A Choice of Evils (1995)

Other novels
The Clock That Wouldn't
 Stop (1952)

Murder in Time (1953)
The Lying Voices (1954)
Enough to Kill a Horse (1955)
Murder Moves In (1956)
 aka *Kill or Cure*
We Haven't Seen Her Lately
 (1956)
 aka *Always Say Die*
Furnished for Murder (1957)
Unreasonable Doubt (1958)
 aka *Count the Cost*
Fear the Light (1960)
The Sleeping Dogs (1960)
The Doubly Dead (1963)
A Legal Fiction (1964)
 aka *The Decayed Gentlewoman*
Ninth Life (1965)
No Peace for the Wicked (1966)
The Swaying Pillars (1968)
Hanged Man's House (1974)
The Cup and the Lip (1975)
Experiment with Death (1981)
Skeleton in Search of a
 Cupboard (1982)
Seeing is Believing (1994)
A Thief in the Night (1995)

We Haven't Seen Her Lately

Elizabeth Ferrars

An Orion book

Copyright © Peter MacTaggart 1956

The right of Elizabeth Ferrars to be identified as the author of this work has
been asserted in accordance with the Copyright, Designs and Patents Act 1988.

This edition published by
The Orion Publishing Group Ltd
Orion House
5 Upper St Martin's Lane
London WC2H 9EA

An Hachette UK company
A CIP catalogue record for this book is available from the British Library

ISBN 978 1 4719 0702 9

www.orionbooks.co.uk

To Jo and Adrian
with love

I

IN THE dim light of the staircase Helen Gamlen did not recognise the man standing on the half-landing below her. She thought that his ringing her bell had probably been a mistake and that he was looking for someone in one of the other flats.

She said inquiringly, " Yes ? "

But, as she waited, she realised that he was taking a curiously long time to make up his mind to answer. He was looking up at her intently, making no move to continue up the stairs.

Suddenly a suspicion came to her that he was remaining deliberately in the shadows, where she could hardly see him.

" Whom do you want ? " she asked more sharply.

His scrutiny of her out of the shadows ended with a laugh.

" I was afraid that you might not be glad to see me," he said, " but I never thought——"

" Martin ! "

Her heart pounded. Taking a step forward, she stood peering down at him with a wondering stare.

She saw that he had changed very little in three years. His thin, brown face was still as vividly expressive. His dark eyes, bright as ever, were still as arrogant. It seemed impossible now that she should have failed to recognise him, even momentarily and in the near-darkness of the landing. Yet something in her held on to a doubt of his identity and wanted intensely to hold on to that doubt.

Martin Andras put a foot on the next stair. " Aren't you going to let me in ? " he asked.

" Of course," she said. " But you took me by surprise, Martin. For a moment I couldn't believe it."

" And after all, why should you, after all this time ? Why don't you say that too, Helen ? "

She managed to smile with a look of false calm. " Are

1

we going to quarrel even now ? Is that what you've come for ? "

" No," he said, coming up the stairs towards her. " But you looked—yes, standing there looking down at me, you looked as if you hated me. And that took me by surprise too. I thought that by now I could count on your having no feelings about me whatever."

" Perhaps that's rather much to have expected." She turned towards her door.

" If you don't want me to come in," he said, " I can stay here. There's something I have to ask you, but it'll take only a few minutes. Then I can go away again."

" Is that what you'd prefer ? "

" If it were, should I have come at all ? " he asked. " I'd have telephoned or written a letter."

" Then come in," she said. " Now that I'm getting over the surprise, I'm very glad to see you. And if you'd thought of telephoning to warn me that you were coming, you could have avoided seeing the effects of shock."

" If I'd telephoned, you might have told me not to come," he said.

He followed her into the flat. There was still a suddenness, impulsive but uncertain, in his movements, that gave his slender but powerfully built body a kind of boyishness, though by now he was at least thirty.

Walking towards the gas fire that had been installed in the square Georgian fireplace, he held out his hands to it, then turned and looked thoughtfully about the room. It was a high room with tall windows, covered by long, pearl-grey curtains and with tall double doors at one end that led into Helen's bedroom. The walls were covered in panelling, painted white. All the colours were pale and cool, except for the crimson of some dahlias in a glass bowl on a low table and the bright bindings of the books on the shelves.

Helen herself looked pale and cool. She was fair, grey-eyed and small, dressed in the grey suit in which she had just returned from the art-school, where she had recently started teaching. But just now there was an unusual brightness in her cheeks.

2

Going to a cupboard, she took out a decanter and two glasses.

"Sherry, Martin? I'm afraid it's all I can offer you."

He nodded, his eyes on the movements of her hands.

She went on, "You said you wanted to ask me something."

She could think of nothing that he could genuinely need to ask her, since their lives no longer touched at any point.

"Now that I'm here," he said, "there are lots of things I want to ask you."

"But there was some particular thing?"

"Oh yes. I'll tell you about that presently. But first I want to ask how things are going with you. You've a job at an art-school?"

"Yes."

"D'you like it?"

"Well enough. And you, Martin? Architecture's paying off quite well, isn't it? I saw the designs that won you that competition." She handed him a glass of sherry. "I was impressed."

He looked as if he had not heard what she said. He was still watching her intently, his dark, bright eyes following carefully the motion of her hand as she lifted her glass to her lips.

She remembered this way he had of seeming to listen very little to what was said to him, though afterwards, in one way and another, it appeared that he had heard it all.

"Well," she said, sitting down in a low chair near the fire, "what else can I tell you?"

He said abruptly, "You aren't married?"

"Didn't you see the same old name on the doorbell?"

"That doesn't always mean much, these days."

"Well then—no, I'm not. And you?"

"No."

"That," she said, staring down into her glass, "surprises me a little."

"Why?" he asked. "When you remember the things you said to me about myself the last time we were

3

together, why should you be surprised that another woman wouldn't risk marrying me ? "

" The things *I* said . . . ? "

" Don't you remember them ? I've never been able to get the sound of them out of my head. And when I saw you on the stairs just now with that look on your face, I thought, God, she still hates me as much as ever, she'll never get over hating me."

" I never hated you," she said. " And if you don't go on trying to pick a quarrel with me, I won't start now."

" *I* pick a quarrel . . . ? "

Helen began to laugh.

For a moment his gaze on her face remained brooding and concentrated, then he laughed too, and looking round, for a chair, settling himself, said, " Honestly, the last thing I'd have thought, when I decided to come here, was that we could possibly quarrel. I'd never have thought that we had it in us any more. Three years is a long time, you know."

" What happened ? " Helen asked. " Why didn't you marry her ? "

" Do I have to talk about it ? "

" I feel a certain curiosity."

" Suppose I satisfy it some other time, then, when I've got a little more used to you."

" Is there going to be another time ? "

He raised an eyebrow. " All right," he said, " why shouldn't I talk about it ? Haven't you realised yet that that marriage was entirely your own idea ? No one but you ever thought it was going to happen."

" That isn't true," she said. " Myra told me——"

" Ah," he said, " Myra. But I didn't think that even you believed it. I thought—don't you know what I thought, Helen ? "

" No, and perhaps after all I don't really want to know. Suppose you tell me now what it was that you came here to ask me."

" Oh, that," he said. " That was just something about your aunt, Mrs. Colliver."

" Aunt Violet ? " she said in a startled voice.

4

But the look of inattention was back on his face, the look of having absorbing thoughts of his own to pursue, of not hearing what was said to him.

"You know, I really did believe, when I decided to come here, that I didn't mean to start us talking about ourselves," he said. "But that may have been self-deception. I may just have waited for a good enough excuse to come and see you. I'd wanted for a long time, for my own satisfaction, to find out why things happened as they did. I never believed in that jealousy of yours, I thought it was just a pretext for getting away."

"Martin!" Leaning forward, she raised her voice a little. "What do you want to know about Aunt Violet?"

"I want to know whether you've any reason to think she's alive," he said. "But listen, Helen, seeing you on the stairs just now with that look on your face, it seemed to me all of a sudden that I could have been wrong. That that jealousy could have been real, that you could actually have believed all those things you said. And in that case . . ." He made a small gesture with one hand as if he were brushing something away from him. "In that case, I could have spared myself a lot of misery, just by using my head."

Helen stood up. It was a swift movement and she followed it by a few steps across the room, but then stood still.

She was warning herself not to listen too carefully to what Martin was saying, or to look at him more than she could help. The mere sight of him stirred her as much as it ever had.

"Whyever shouldn't Aunt Violet be alive?" she asked.

He frowned as if he found this an irresponsible change of subject. "You haven't heard anything special about her, then?" he said.

"No, but I should have if anything had happened to her."

"Are you sure?"

"Of course I am. That is . . . Well . . ." She came back to stand before the fireplace, looking down at him.

" What *has* happened to her ? You've come here to tell me something, haven't you, not to ask me anything ? "

For a moment his inattentive look persisted, but then he seemed reluctantly to accept the necessity of talking about this subject that he himself had raised.

" Does it surprise you," he said, " to hear that she hasn't been seen in the village for more than a year ? "

It did surprise Helen very much. Her aunt, Mrs. Colliver, had lived in the village of Burnstone in Berkshire for thirty years. For twenty-five of those years she had been housekeeper to Martin's grandfather, Laurence Delborne, and on his death she had continued to live in his house, which he had left her, together with a surprisingly large income, for her lifetime. It had always seemed certain that she would live there till she died.

However, Aunt Violet was capable of doing unexpected things. At the age of fifty-seven, two years after the death of old Mr. Delborne, she had gone on a holiday to Bournemouth and had returned with a husband, Elvin Colliver. After that it had never seemed quite possible to take her behaviour for granted.

" What are you suggesting, Martin ? " Helen asked.

" I'm not suggesting anything," he said. " I came simply to find out if you knew anything about her. I'll explain why. You remember some people in Burnstone called Hindmarch ? "

" Yes. They lived in a white house with some wistaria on it. Quite kind, but awful busy-bodies."

" Yes. Well, a fortnight ago Mrs. Hindmarch wrote to my mother, saying she'd heard that Uncle Laurence's house would come to her on Mrs. Colliver's death, and that therefore perhaps she'd be interested to hear that the property was going to rack and ruin. Mrs. Hindmarch being as you described her, Mother was inclined not to bother about the letter, but then, on further thought, she sent me down to find out what it was all about."

" But Aunt Violet would never neglect that house ! " Helen said.

" I told you, Mrs. Colliver hasn't been seen in Burnstone for over a year," Martin said. "Colliver and a sister of his live there on their own. And the house itself, as a matter of fact, wasn't in too bad a state. It needed some paint and a few odd repairs, that's all. But the mess inside the house, the squalor of it, and the state of the garden——I'm not excessively critical about domestic things, but I almost fled from that place, Helen. Apart from the dirt, there are cats all over the place and a pet snake and a smell you could cut with a knife. And there are thistles as tall as myself in the rosebeds and the lawn's produced a nice crop of rotting hay."

"It's incredible," Helen said.

"It would be if your aunt were around," he answered. "But she isn't."

"And so—and so you actually think——" She could not finish the sentence.

"Let's face it," Martin said. "If your aunt were to die, the Collivers would have to give up the house and a steady income too to my mother. Rather than do that, they might prefer to conceal her death. And don't say that's incredible. Once you've seen Miss Colliver and met her tame rattlesnake and been rapped and tapped at by some of the tame spooks she keeps in the house, and encountered the cobwebs and the smell, you'll be ready to believe she's capable of anything. I'm not joking, Helen. I came back really worried about your aunt."

"Didn't you ask the Collivers where she was?"

"Of course. And they said she was away on a visit."

"No details?"

"None."

"All the same," Helen said, "I'm sure Aunt Violet's all right. I had a postcard from her sometime in the summer."

"Are you sure that the postcard came from your aunt?"

She gave an exclamation of exasperation. "Martin, what's the matter with you? Are you *looking* for trouble?"

He did not answer immediately. Emptying his glass,

he set it down and again thrust his hands towards the gas-fire. Instead of looking up at Helen, he looked down at his hands.

"Listen," he said, "I've an idea you may have leapt to a conclusion about this interest of mine in your aunt. As I said just now, if she were dead, that house, which I suppose would sell for five or six thousand pounds, besides that nice steady income of a thousand or so, would come to my mother. And she could do with both, of course. I'm not trying to deceive you about that. All the same, I came here not to get you to help me to prove that Mrs. Colliver's dead, but in the hope that you could reassure me that she's still alive."

"You didn't need to explain that." Helen picked up his empty glass and refilled both it and her own. "But I did have a postcard from Aunt Violet a couple of months ago. A picture-postcard. I think it came from Torquay. I've probably got it somewhere. And apart from that, I can't help remembering that you always had a leaning to drama."

"Do you think you could find the postcard?"

Helen shrugged her shoulders and turned towards a bureau in a corner of the room.

She realised, as she did so, that she did not want to produce the card. She could not have said quite why, but she had a feeling that by producing it she would in some way be playing into Martin's hands. He had some purpose in these questions which so far he had kept to himself. She knew him too well to have missed the signs of this. The tension of those long, finely-modelled hands that he was still holding out to the fire, together with his unwillingness at first to tell her what he had come to ask her, followed by his insistence on talking about it, made her feel certain that his interest in her Aunt Violet was not as simple as it appeared.

Not that Helen doubted his statement that he had no special impatience for his mother to inherit his uncle's house and money. Such a feeling would have been too uncomplicated for Martin. Besides, there was no greed in him. Unless he had changed deeply in three years, possessions were almost abnormally unimportant to him.

She saw the postcard in a corner of a drawer of the bureau, protruding from a heap of old letters. As her hand touched it, she had an impulse to thrust it out of sight under the scattered papers. But her own curiosity made her draw it out.

It was an ordinary picture-postcard, showing a view of Torquay. On the back of it was written, " Having a lovely time here. Why don't you come and join me, dear ? I'm at the Green Mount Residential Hotel, ever so comfortable, and I'll be here a month or so. Do come if you have time. Love from your old Auntie."

Martin reached for the card with one of his sudden movements.

" It does look like her writing," he said.

" Of course it does," Helen said.

" You didn't think of going ? "

" No, I'd made plans to go to the South of France."

" Did you answer the card ? "

" I sent her one—from Avignon, I think—not to the hotel, but to Burnstone. I thought she'd probably have gone home already."

" And you've heard nothing since ? "

" No, but I'd never expect it. Picture-postcards on holidays and birthday cards and Christmas-cards form nearly the whole of Aunt Violet's correspondence."

Martin turned the card over and seemed to study carefully the view of hotel roofs and tree-covered cliffs. Then he looked back once more at the few lines in Violet Colliver's rounded, not quite educated writing.

" A month or so," he said thoughtfully. " That means she might still be there."

" Do you know what I think ? " Helen said.

He did not answer, but went on looking at the card. There was no sign that he was listening to her.

Helen went on, " If it's true that she hasn't been seen in Burnstone for a year and is paying quite long visits to seaside hotels, it looks as if marriage to Elvin Colliver hasn't turned out all that she'd hoped, and being the gentle creature that she is, instead of putting up a struggle to push him out of her house, she's quietly gone away herself and stayed away as much as she could."

Martin still did not answer. Without making any comment on what she had said, he was glancing about the room. Then he asked, " Do you mind if I use your telephone ? "

" Go ahead."

He began by ringing up Directory Inquiries, then, with the information he obtained, he rang up the Green Mount Residential Hotel in Torquay. When a voice answered him, he asked two or three questions, then put the telephone down again.

" Well, that's that," he said.

There was a finality in his tone that made Helen's heart lurch.

" What is it ? " she asked sharply.

He came slowly back to the fireplace.

" She was at the Green Mount until about a fortnight ago. At least, a woman was there who answers to her description. When she left, she gave a forwarding address, Shipley's End, Burnstone."

Exasperated again, Helen exclaimed, " And I thought from the way you spoke that she must be dead at least ! Martin, what *is* the matter with you ? Why are you trying to create a drama out of poor Aunt Violet ? She leaves a hotel and she gives her own home as a forwarding address—whatever's the matter with that ? "

" A drama ? " he said savagely, coming abruptly out of his private world to stare at her with anger. " Don't you understand even now what I'm trying to say to you. *She hasn't been seen in Burnstone for more than a year!* And Colliver . . . Who's Colliver ? Who knows anything about him, except that he certainly married her for her money ? And that garden, Helen—that garden with thistles six foot high and docks and brambles. . . Wouldn't that be an easy place to hide a body, Helen ? "

10

II

HE LEFT soon after that. Helen had treated his suggestion with contempt and after a moment he himself had laughed at it. Yet his laughter had not been quite convincing. It had been as if he had decided to humour her in her obtruseness.

In the doorway, as he was leaving, he had laid his hands on her shoulders.

" No ? " he had said, one eyebrow lifted.

She had hesitated, then had lifted her face. He had touched her cheek lightly with his lips, then gone away. Neither of them had said anything of seeing the other again.

Shutting the door after him, Helen went slowly back to the fireplace and stood there, looking unseeingly at the white wall above it.

Martin's professed fears for her aunt did not disturb her. Mrs. Colliver could hardly be dead and buried under the thistles in Burnstone and at the same time have spent a comfortable summer at Torquay. What did disturb Helen was the fact that she could make no guess at Martin's reasons for trying to work on her fears with a theory so absurd and unconvincing. His hints that the woman at the Green Mount Residential Hotel might have been an impostor and the postcard a forgery seemed quite senseless. For why should an impostor have pressed Helen to visit her ?

Lighting a cigarette, she sat down on the hearthrug. Her face felt scorched by the heat from the hissing gas jets. It reddened her cheeks and made them tingle. Could it be, she wondered, that Martin's purpose had been no more than to make his way back into some relationship with her ?

Three years ago it had taken all Helen's strength of will to break off that relationship. It had been much too stormy for her, too uncertain, too full of distrust.

She had felt as if it were turning her into someone who was not like her real self. And now, as she stared at the glowing rectangle of the fire and saw in her mind's eye Martin's thin, dark, vivid face, the sense of the same threat returned.

The time that had followed the break had been agonising and full of regrets that she had not wholly expected, though in the main she had been glad that she had found the courage to act as she had. But at the thought of going through anything of the same kind again, she shrank in horror. And unless there had been great changes in Martin, far greater than those that had taken place in herself, it was certain to come to the same thing in the end.

The trouble was that the relationship went back so far and was woven so deeply into both their lives that she did not really believe that it would ever be possible to escape from it entirely.

It went back to that summer, fifteen years ago, when death had poured out of the sky on to London and old Mr. Delborne had suggested to his housekeeper, Miss Gamlen, that Burnstone might be a healthier place than Streatham for the young niece whose photographs decorated her sitting-room and whose not particularly remarkable exploits, to the old man's intense irritation, had always filled a large part of Miss Gamlen's conversation. At the same time he had written to his niece, Martin's mother, whom he had never liked and had always kept at a distance, suggesting that Martin should spend his holidays with him, instead of in Kensington. Then, his good deed done, Mr. Delborne had retired into his study, demanding most of his meals on trays, and had gone on quietly writing his many-volumed work on the life and times of the Emperor Julian. Both the children had developed lasting feelings of respect for this remarkable emperor, since he had been capable of keeping the mind of such a terrifying grown-up as Mr. Delborne so fully occupied that he had hardly ever got in their way.

Helen had loved Martin at sight. All of a sudden, it

had seemed, she had been given that for which she had most longed, a brother, and this brother had arrived in the form of a long-legged, handsome boy, two years older than herself, with a spirit so adventurous and an imagination so original that it had seemed to her probable that there was no one else like him in the world. She had given her heart instantly. Martin had accepted the gift with pleasure and had made considerable use of it, though just how much of his own he had given in return she had never known. That was not a question that in those days had seemed to matter. His company, during the wonderful weeks of his school holidays, and her own devotion had been enough to give her a year of happiness.

But the bombing had stopped and parents had grown restless to have their children at home. Helen and Martin had been separated. For a while they had written to one another and sent each other birthday presents, then the time had come when they heard no more of each other except in Miss Gamlen's occasional letters. Through these Helen had known when Martin had gone into the army and when he had decided to become an architect. But it had not been until she was nineteen and had gone to an art school, that she had met him again. He had been a student in the department of architecture attached to the same school, a brilliant student, one of the most promising. He had also been deep in a love-affair.

There had always been other women round Martin. And Helen had been jealous, not very much at first, while her own claims were still slight, but later on, after he had returned from America, where he had studied for two years, coming to see her again as unexpectedly as he had come this evening, the feeling had become an obsession.

Staring before her with eyes that were smarting a little from the dry heat of the fire, she thought how wrong he had been this evening when he had suggested that her jealousy had not been real, but only a pretext for getting away from him. She had been hopelessly, miserably jealous of him. Her whole nature had become clogged by jealousy. And more than any of the others, she had been jealous of his beautiful, possessive mother, Myra Andras.

As she thought of it, Helen made a curious fierce little gesture. She remembered how her love had seemed to fade into a quiet, frightened bitterness. Her own fault, probably, but what did that matter now?

What mattered was that she should never return to such a state of mind. And so perhaps it would be best not to concern herself too much with Martin's real purpose in coming to see her, but to start thinking about Aunt Violet, her only surviving relative, since her own mother had died two years before. Poor Aunt Violet, who appeared to have found her late love as unsatisfactory as Helen had found her early one. Might not Martin be right in thinking that it was high time for someone to start worrying a little about Violet Colliver?

By the following Saturday, Helen had done enough worrying to feel that at least she might pay a visit to Shipley's End and make some inquiries. Packing an overnight case, she caught a morning train to Oxford, and then a bus which, after about an hour, would deliver her at the Old Swan in Burnstone. Before starting, she had telephoned and reserved a room there, but apart from that had warned no one of her coming.

As the bus, stopping every few hundred yards, made its slow way along the quiet lanes, Helen found herself wondering why she had not come long before, but this thought had very little to do with Aunt Violet. It came from the soft light of the October afternoon, falling on the yellowing hedges, and on gardens filled with all the flowers of autumn, dahlias, chrysanthemums, michaelmas daisies, tall perennial sunflowers, and late roses, and bringing out the faint golden tinge in the grey stone of small thatched cottages.

The sky was a pale, hazy blue, quite cloudless. It showed through the high branches of tall trees, covered now only in a light coppery transparency of leaves, while those that had fallen lay in moist, darkening drifts in the ditches. At each turn in the lane there was some fresh loveliness to be seen. Helen felt all the surprise of the town-dweller, to whom autumn is merely the indistinct merging of the fading end of summer and the beginning of winter. But here it had an identity of its own, shining and delicate.

The Old Swan was at one end of the single street that composed the village of Burnstone. The building was set at an odd angle, so that one of its corners jutted out into the street. It was of the usual grey stone with a roof of moss-grown slates, but was by no means a simple country inn. It had central heating, a good restaurant and high prices. Expensive cars were to be seen in its courtyard.

As Helen entered the lobby the manager came forward and shook her enthusiastically by the hand. He was a short, plump man with a square, pink, snub-nosed face and thick, bristling grey hairs. He wore a pale grey suit, perfectly pressed, with a snowy handkerchief jutting from the cuff. He had once been an actor, specialising in horrific parts, but had had a nervous breakdown and been told that he should retire to the country. The Swan had been as far as he had felt able to go in pursuing a country life.

" Such a nice surprise, Miss Gamlen, seeing you here," he said. " It's years since you've been to the old place. How are you and how is Mrs. Colliver? I haven't seen her for a long time. She's been visiting you, perhaps. Is she well? A wonderful old lady. She's very well, I hope."

His eyes were bright with an eager curiosity, a lust, almost, for gossip.

Helen answered, " Thanks, Bertie. I'm sure she's very well."

His name was Bertram Wilbraham, and in the village he was generally known as Bertie.

" You want to see your room? " he said. " I've given you a lovely one. I had it done last spring with Regency stripes. Old-fashioned already, of course, but still so charming. We're very busy, but I've given you one of our best rooms. Then you'd like tea, perhaps? "

"Later, I think," Helen said. "I want to go out first."

"Good, good, whenever you wish. And your uncle, Mr. Colliver, is he well too? He never comes here. An abstainer, I'm afraid. But I see him in the village. We mention the weather, and sometimes we discuss the life after death. A very interesting man."

"You discuss the life after death in the middle of the street in Burnstone!" Helen exclaimed. "Are you making it up, Bertie?"

"No, no, no!" He waved one of his plump hands. "We talk shop, that's all. It's his shop, didn't you know? Spiritualism and all that."

He rang a bell and a maid appeared to take Helen up to her room.

It was a big room that had originally been part of an even bigger one. The mouldings on the ceiling disappeared into the blank partition wall to reappear, presumably, in the room next door. The Regency stripes were crimson and white and at least one piece of furniture in the room looked like a genuine antique. Helen put down her case, took off her hat, ran a comb through her hair and touched up her mouth with lipstick. Then she lit a cigarette and went to look out of the window.

She was worried by Bertie's curiosity about her aunt, more worried, in fact, than she had been by Martin's. For if Aunt Violet had merely separated from her husband, however quietly, however discreetly, this for certain would somehow have become known in the village and Bertie would have had the tact not to refer to the matter at all until Helen had revealed her own knowledge of it.

From where she stood, she could see the roof of Shipley's End, deep red against the deep green of some pines that rose behind it, making a spiky pattern along the edge of the tranquil, hazy sky. Everything at that distance looked as it always had. There appeared to have been few changes in Burnstone, though a semi-circle of harshly bright roofs behind some concealing trees, suggested the presence of a new council estate, built probably to house the workers at Burnstone's one factory.

With a sigh, Helen turned from the window and went downstairs. In the hall she met Bertie again. He appeared to have been waiting for her.

"Forgive the question," he said, "but are you going now to visit Mr. and Miss Colliver?"

"Yes," she said.

"And—and do you think you'll come back to dinner?"

Something in his eyes told Helen that this had not been the question that he had intended to ask when he started to speak, but that for some reason his courage had failed him.

At the same time she was aware that a man who was sitting in the small lounge that opened out of the hall, with a tea-tray on a table beside him, had raised his head and was looking at her intently.

"Oh, I expect so," she said.

"It's a very good dinner to-night," Bertie said. "Steak. Best Scots beef. If I'm sure you're coming I'll save some for you."

The man in the lounge was a big man of heavy build, aged about forty. His brown hair was flecked with grey. He had a weatherbeaten face and very clear, light blue eyes. He wore an old tweed jacket, flannel trousers and heavy shoes which still had mud caked on to them, as if he had just come in from a country walk.

"Thanks," Helen said, "then I'll certainly come back."

"Yes, and——" Bertie hesitated for a second again. "Yes, and first come and have a drink with me, Miss Gamlen. Have a drink and we'll talk about old times. You won't forget that?"

Helen thanked him again and went out quickly.

The afternoon sun had sunk so low as she walked along the village street that the light shone straight into her eyes and dazzled her. With its sinking, the air had grown colder. Buttoning her light tweed coat up to her neck, she buried her hands in her pockets, thinking that this phase of autumn, with its tinge of gold in everything and its warm, sweet scents, could vanish at any moment now in a few gusts of bitter wind. The last leaves would be whirled away and winter would be upon them.

Walking fast, she wondered how soon she could get through this visit that she must make, and return to have that drink with Bertie. She was sure that he had something to tell her which concerned her aunt, and perhaps the Collivers. Helen had met Elvin Colliver only once, soon after her aunt, with an air of demure and slightly bewildered triumph, had brought him back from Bournemouth as her husband. Helen had been invited to Burnstone for a week-end. It had passed off quite pleasantly and though Helen had found in herself a regret for the change of order at Shipley's End, she had criticised herself for this, rather than Elvin Colliver. Nevertheless, she had not really been sorry when no more invitations had come.

She reached the house just as the sun, looking suddenly enormous, began to dip beneath the horizon. Standing by the gate, she paused to watch it. The sun seemed just then to be moving so fast that there was something unnatural, almost frightening in the moment. It was as if some control had slipped.

Immediately afterwards there was a sharp change in the quality of the remaining light. All the gold went out of it and the calm and stillness of the evening became bleak and a little dismal. Pushing open the gate, Helen started up the short drive to the house, and so saw the garden in that first moment of shadow.

The sight of it made her catch her breath. Nettles had sprouted thickly along the edges of the drive. In the rose-beds the dead spikes of tall thistles overtopped the bushes. The lawn had vanished under long grass and weeds. In the borders a few michaelmas daisies straggled limply among brambles and thistles, with flopping, faded hollyhocks behind them, beaten down by the winds. The drive was grass-grown. The feeling of decay was overpowering.

Just then Helen was ready to accept the wildest of Martin's suggestions, partly because it seemed impossible to believe that such neglect as she saw here could have been anything but deliberate. With anger rising in her, fanned by a sharp gust of apprehension, she looked at the house.

It was a long, low house, grey-walled, red-roofed, a quiet-looking house that had stood there solidly, unpretentiously, through three centuries. The door stood open and a man was waiting in the doorway, watching Helen's approach. As she came face to face with him he held out both hands and caught hold of one of hers, clasping it warmly and eagerly.

"Helen—my dear Helen!" he exclaimed. "What a surprise and what a pleasure!"

Later Helen found that this greeting had made a curious impression upon her. For no reason that she could name, it left her with the conviction that Elvin Colliver was not in the least surprised at her appearance, yet that he was in fact extremely sincere in saying that he was glad to see her.

III

ELVIN COLLIVER was a smallish man of about fifty-five. Though he was not actually fat, there was a look of softness all over him that made him seem padded in pale flesh that would yield like downy quilting wherever it was prodded. His low, rounded forehead, his smooth white cheeks, his little dimpled chin and the narrow circle of his neck that showed above the loose collar of his flannel shirt, all seemed to have this evenly distributed covering. His fairly wide shoulders, inside the dusty-looking brown velvet jacket that he was wearing, looked as if they were weighed down into a stoop by their load of plumpness. His hair was still dark but was sparse, parted low over one ear and smoothed with care across the top of his head. His eyes were prominent, dark, earnest and emotional. His voice was high in pitch, but ringing and clear.

19

In this fine tenor voice, as he stood in the stone-paved hall, still holding on to Helen's hand, he told her, " I am so very, very delighted, my dear. It means so very, very much to me. And dear Violet, how very, very delighted she will be too ! "

" She's here ? " Helen asked.

" No, she's away on a visit," he answered, " but of course I shall write to her and tell her all about your coming. She's so fond of you, as you know, so interested in all that you do. It'll really gladden her heart to know that you wanted to come here. I'll write and—I tell you what, my dear ! " He gave her hand an extra squeeze and beamed with happiness. " You shall add a post-script to the letter. What about that ? Now come in and meet my sister. My sister Mignon."

Still clinging to her hand, he drew her towards the door of the drawing-room.

By this time Helen had become aware of the smell that Martin had described. It was mostly, she thought, the smell of damp, as if too few fires had been lit recently in the old house and too few windows opened. But damp was not the whole of it. It was a complex smell, with sour, animal overtones. Helen had also observed the dusty look of the rugs on the stone flags and the cobwebs hanging from the beamed ceiling. There were even cobwebs spinning together some shrivelled autumn leaves in a tall vase on a table by the wall.

In the old days there had always been fresh flowers in that same vase on that table, and its deep brown mahogany had had the lovely surface that came from tireless care. Now, like everything else, it was smeared and neglected.

As Helen entered the drawing-room with Elvin Colliver, a small woman in a loose purple knitted dress came hurrying across the room to meet her. She had the same trick as her brother of seizing one of her visitor's hands in both of her own and holding on tightly. But her grip, instead of being soft and warm, was rigid and cold and her bones crushed Helen's fingers. Her body was as bony as her brother's was plump, her skin had a grey look, her hurried movements were clumsy and nervous. Her eyes, protuberant like his, were grey, with a singularly clear, glassy brilliance.

Fixing them on Helen's, she said in a breathless murmur, " I know who you are. Even if I hadn't heard Elvin say your name out there in the hall, I'd have known who you were. I'm like that. I find myself knowing the most extraordinary things, without in the least knowing where the knowledge comes from."

To this Helen replied lamely, " I hope I haven't come at an inconvenient time."

" Not inconvenient—never inconvenient—not even surprising," Mignon Colliver said in the same excited, confidential murmur. " To me not in the least surprising. To tell the truth, very few things surprise me, except, all the time, this peculiar power I have of knowing things. That always surprises me and makes me feel very humble. Do you understand that ? Humility's the key to everything. I know that if I lost it, I should instantly lose the power. Now come to the fire and get warm, child. Your hand's cold—quite cold."

To Helen it had seemed that it was the rigid, bony hand clutching hers that was cold, but as it started to tug her towards the small, smoky fire that burnt reluctantly in the big fireplace, the cold seemed to spread into her own.

She could hardly bear to look round her at the room. Associated in her mind with stiff little interviews with Mr. Delborne, on those occasions when he had felt it his duty to show some interest in the two children staying in his house, the drawing-room had always intimidated her, making her dread to find her own fingermarks on the fine damask of the chairs and mud from her shoes on the polished floor. Yet she had cherished her memory of it as a place that had a positive beauty which naturally made unusual demands on those who were privileged to enter it. There had been an excitement, sitting there drinking tea in overawed silence with the old man, in trying to achieve a grace and dignity of manner worthy of the grace and dignity of the room.

Now the only excitement she could feel was in the attempt to avoid tripping over the objects that littered the floor as she made her way to the fire. There was an enamelled iron kettle, balanced on a pile of books. There was a basket of mending, from the appearance of which it seemed that Miss Colliver believed in the theory that socks should be darned before, rather than after being washed. There was a brush and comb. There was a dusty-looking typewriter. There were a great many old newspapers and there was what Helen took at first to be a dog-whip lying across the floor between two chairs and looking almost as if it had been left there on purpose to trip someone up.

As Helen stepped over it, this object suddenly writhed and she cried out.

Mignon Colliver made a swift pounce and gathered up in her arms a snake about a yard long. With a movement of extraordinary sensuality, she coiled it round one of her arms.

"Don't be afraid of him," she said. "Don't be a bit afraid. He's absolutely harmless—and so beautiful, don't you think? . . . Elvin, tea!"

"Please don't bother about tea," Helen said quickly. "I don't want to trouble you at all."

"Trouble?" Elvin Colliver said. "How can you say that? Why, this house was almost a home to you once. You must never, never act as if you felt yourself a visitor here. You must go on feeling just as you used to about this dear old place."

"But, I—I've a friend waiting for me at the Swan," Helen lied rapidly. "I promised I'd be back for tea."

"The Swan?" he said. "You don't mean you're staying the night and have actually taken a room at the Swan instead of coming straight here? That isn't what you mean, is it?"

His glowing dark eyes looked so hurt that Helen felt unreasonably guilty.

"But I couldn't have planted myself on you without any warning," she said. "And I only came to——"

"Tea!" Mignon Colliver interrupted. "There's

some cake in the tin on the shelf beside the shoe-polish, Elvin."

"But really I did promise I'd be back," Helen said, clinging desperately to her lie. "I just came to ask——"

"I know, about your dear aunt," he said. "She'll be so glad to hear it. I shall write to her this evening and tell her all about your visit and about how well and lovely you were looking and how kind your inquiries were."

"It's her address I wanted to know," Helen said.

"She's staying at the Etherfield Guest-house, Burtonlea, Hampshire. Telephone number, Burtonlea 233. You could ring her up immediately if you'd care to. I'm sure that would give her great happiness. Why don't you do that while I'm getting the tea?"

Before Helen could protest, he ran out of the room.

Helplessly, she sat down. There was at least some reassurance to be found in the fact that she had been given her aunt's address without any reluctance, but she disliked the idea of telephoning from that room, with Miss Colliver listening to her.

Miss Colliver, whose clear, grey, glassy eyes had never left Helen's face, leant forward slightly now and said, "I suppose you don't take me seriously."

Feeling unable to answer, Helen said nothing.

Miss Colliver went on, "About my power. About what an extraordinary thing it is to possess. About how important it is to use it rightly. Of course I realise that it isn't actually my own power at all. I'm simply a vehicle, a means of communication. And that's never been so clear to me as it has in this house. I've never been in such a wonderful atmosphere, where I felt so absolutely sure of the validity of the communications. . . . Because naturally we all have our doubts, don't we? In this age of science, how could it be otherwise? It's impossible not to wonder sometimes if it isn't just a case of one's own mind getting out of hand, one's unconscious getting out of control. . . . But then I get these flashes of *knowledge*. Truly there's no other word for it. And when I check up afterwards, because even now

23

I feel a great deal of self-distrust . . ." She paused broodingly.

But she seemed not to expect any response, so Helen remained silent and after a moment, the soft, blurry voice went on, " Sometimes I think it's wrong even to check up. It shows a lack of faith. I've discussed it with them, but the answers have been rather bewildering. They often are, you know, that's quite characteristic. One does one's best to interpret, but one's so fallible oneself, one may utterly misunderstand."

" Whom did you say you'd discussed it with ? " Helen asked, feeling impelled to clarify something at least.

" My controls," Miss Colliver answered simply. She gave a vague look round the room. " I've got their answers somewhere, just as I wrote them down. I could show them to you, if I could remember just where . . . Really, I'd be very glad to know what you think."

" I'm afraid I know nothing at all about these things," Helen said.

" Ah. But you did know Mr. Delborne, didn't you ? "

Helen stirred uneasily in her chair. She noticed that its damask was covered with greasy spots and that a hole had been burnt in it by a cigarette-end. A tuft of soiled stuffing had worked its way through the hole.

" As a child I did," she said.

" There's nothing like a child's memory," Miss Colliver said, a new eagerness coming into her voice. " Tell me—please tell me, but only if you know it for certain, of your own knowledge—don't say anything just because you think it will please me—did Mr. Delborne always keep a spare pair of spectacles in the drawer of his bedside table, along with a small book covered in red leather ? "

" I'm sorry, I don't know," Helen said. " I don't believe I ever went into his bedroom."

" I see. Yes, I see . . . naturally. You wouldn't, of course. But Violet would know, wouldn't she ? She'd be certain to know. Are you thinking of going to see Violet, child ? Is that why you wanted her address ? "

"Yes, I was thinking of it," Helen said.

"Soon?"

"As soon as I can."

"Then will you ask her that—just what I've asked you —and let me know the answer? Will you do that?" The murmuring voice was almost trembling with excitement. "*Please?*"

Helen would have liked to have the courage to refuse, but it was easier to give the promise. A moment later Elvin Colliver came back into the room, carrying a kitchen tray loaded with an odd mixture of spode and utility cups, an aluminium teapot, a milk-bottle and a plate of very stale-looking currant cake. Helen found that after the time she had spent alone with his sister, his presence seemed almost healthy and normal.

She did not manage to escape for nearly another hour. So far as she was able to judge, both the Collivers were perfectly sincere in their pleasure at seeing her. They seemed equally pleased that she should visit her aunt. Elvin Colliver repeated his suggestion that Helen should use the telephone to speak to her immediately and also repeated his invitation that she should spend the night at the house, seeming hurt when she again refused. When she rose to go, he went with her to the door and opening it wide, looked out into the garden.

"It gets dark so early now," he said, "I'll walk along with you."

"No, really—I know every inch of the way," she answered.

He gave her an odd look. "You'd sooner go alone? . . . But you'll come again, won't you, Helen? You know, I understand how you feel about Mignon and me, I really do. And when young Andras was here, I understood quite well how he was feeling. It must have been quite a shock for all Violet's relations when she married. At her age. . . . Well, I'd expected to be looked over with a little suspicion, but I'd hoped you'd get over it and even come to like me. But, well . . ." He gave a resigned little laugh and laid a soft hand on Helen's shoulder. "Why not try once more and see if we're

25

really so bad. I know we're odd people, perhaps too odd for you, perhaps too unattractive, but still . . ."

He said it with a simplicity that affected Helen curiously. All of a sudden she felt that in her revulsion at the squalor in the old house and in her quick dislike of the two queer people living in it, there had been something cheap, something coarse-grained. Perhaps there was some appealing quality in this small, soft-looking man with the emotional eyes that she had missed until now, but which her aunt, with the perception of a simpler and probably warmer heart, had recognised. Perhaps at least there was a pathos which should not go unfelt.

On an impulse, she said, " Mr. Colliver, will you tell me something ? You've spoken this afternoon as if my aunt were away on a visit, an ordinary visit, but I've been told that she hasn't been in Burnstone for a year. Will you tell me why that's happened ? "

At that moment something sprang at Helen out of the darkness. It sprang at her with claws and lashing tail, and hung from her, the claws piercing her clothes, pricking her skin. She gave a sharp cry and stepped backwards, trying wildly to shake the creature off.

Elvin Colliver reached out quietly and plucked it off her. It was a big tortoise-shell cat. Cradled in his arms, it looked quite harmless and Helen heard herself giving a high-pitched laugh.

" How silly of me," she said. But she was trembling and wanted to run away down the drive into the safe, commonplace darkness.

" I'm so sorry," he answered gently. " How that must have startled you. Mignon's so fond of animals, you see, and they all love her, wherever she goes. If she goes out for a walk, some dog always follows her and she's quite uncanny with birds. This big fellow here, we don't know where he came from, he just wandered in and adopted us soon after we arrived. He's handsome, isn't he, but a little wild."

He tossed the cat away from him. It landed with a light thud and shot past him into the house.

" Now," he said, " about your question . . ."

Helen by now was wishing that she had not asked it. She wanted only one thing, to get away quickly. But Elvin Colliver's sad, understanding voice went on.

" I'm glad you brought it out like that, face to face. I knew all the time, of course, that it was what was on your mind, and I've kept wondering whether or not you were going to find the courage to ask it. I'm glad you did, Helen—very glad. But as for the answer . . ."

He paused, then turned in the doorway, as if that were all that he intended to say. But, with his hand on the latch, he added, " I think it's for your aunt to give you the answer herself when you go to see her."

IV

THE SKY was starless and the road, for the first few minutes after Helen left the house, seemed very dark. In spite of her belief that she knew every inch of the way, she felt almost as strange there as on a road in an unfamiliar part of the country. It was as if the changes at Shipley's End had affected far more than the house and garden.

Then she heard voices behind her and some men on bicycles overtook her on her way back to the village. They called out " Good evening " to her as they went by. She supposed they were men from Hovard and Hayle, the factory that produced some well-known pharmaceutical products, on their way home to the new council estate. As their lights went flickering down the road ahead of her and the rough, reassuring sound of their voices drifted back to her, they took the eeriness out of the quiet evening. As her feet crushed through dry leaves, a pleasant nutty scent rose up from them. In a cottage garden a goose cackled and a dog barked. Then the houses of the village, with their lighted windows, drove away the last feeling of strangeness and she began to laugh at herself for having been scared by a cat and at

Martin Andras for having imagined that Aunt Violet could have been murdered.

In the bar at the Old Swan she found Bertie Wilbraham talking to the man whom she had seen having tea by himself in the lounge. There was no one else there except the white-jacketed waiter behind the bar.

Bertie introduced her and his companion to one another, " Mr. Dreydel—Miss Gamlen," then asked them both what they would have to drink. Helen asked for sherry and Mr. Dreydel for a half-pint of bitter. As Bertie passed these requests on to the waiter, he explained further, " Mr. Dreydel's home on holiday from Africa. Miss Gamlen is the niece of Mrs. Colliver."

The man gave a quick smile, as if this piece of information about Helen meant something to him. She looked at him curiously. The smile was gone already, leaving his weather-beaten face grave. The way his clear, light blue eyes were looking at her reminded her of the oddly intent glance that he had given her from the lounge.

" Do you know my aunt, then ? " she asked.

" No, but I've been taking a lot of interest in her house and asking a lot of questions about it," he said. His voice was deep and distinct, pleasant to listen to after the light, ringing tones of Elvin Colliver and his sister's fuzzy murmur. " It's a very beautiful house."

" I've been telling Mr. Dreydel," Bertie said, " it isn't the property of Mrs. Colliver, but of Mrs. Andras, who's the niece of Mr. Delborne, who bought the house thirty— thirty-five years ago from Miss Sarah and Miss Christina and Miss Maria Beaufort, who came over with the Conqueror."

" Yes, that's more or less its history, I believe," Helen said. " Do you know a great deal about old houses, Mr. Dreydel ? "

" Almost nothing at all, but one can always make a beginning," he said. " I've got a few months' leave, and since I didn't really know what else to do with the time, I thought I might as well spend it catching up a little on my knowledge of the country. I've found it rather a shock to discover how little I know about it."

"Then you've been abroad a great deal?" Helping rather absently to keep the conversation going, Helen realised that Bertie, sipping a martini, was looking uneasy and impatient, as if something had happened that he had not intended.

"Off and on, most of my life," Mr. Dreydel said. "Colonial service."

"In the past I travelled a great deal too," Bertie said. "Too much. Now I stay in one place."

The quick smile came again in Dreydel's light blue eyes. He said to Helen, "I believe it would make an interesting story, the history of how our friend came to pick on Burnstone as the place to stay in at last."

"One day I'll tell it," Bertie said in a tone of remarkably false candour, while his uneasy glance, meeting Helen's for an instant, seemed to be trying to give her a message. "One day, when I have time. Now I'm very busy. I've some work to do in my office. You'll excuse me?" Abruptly he emptied his glass, gave a stiff little bow and left them.

For a moment neither Helen nor Dreydel spoke. Then Dreydel laughed.

"I think, you know, he's expecting you, after a decent interval of say one minute, to follow him to his office."

That brought her attention for the first time sharply on to him.

He went on, "I think he wants to warn you about me—that I've really been asking too many questions for an innocent traveller."

She gave herself a moment to think, then asked composedly, "And have you?"

"Far too many."

"About——?" She was suddenly both scared and angry, but determined to show neither feeling. "About that house?"

"And about the people living in it. And this afternoon, when I heard that you were going to see them, about you."

" I suppose," Helen said thoughtfully, " that you mean to tell me what this is all about."

" Don't you think it might be wiser first to hear what Bertie has to tell you ? "

" Probably it would, but since you brought the subject up, may I ask you why you've been asking questions ? "

" Yes, if you'll finish that sherry and let me get you some more."

She hesitated, then picked up her glass and emptied it.

" Well ? " she said a moment later, as he returned from the bar with another glass.

" I'm trying to trace the whereabouts of a certain woman," he said.

" You mean my aunt ? "

" No. A young woman. Her name was Evelyn Lander."

" *Was* ? " she said.

To her surprise, he flushed. It seemed to Helen that there was something strangely incongruous about the sight, making him look a less rugged, more vulnerable character than she thought he had intended to appear.

" I ought not to have said that," he said. " I've no reason to—yet."

" Are you a detective ? " she asked.

" No, I'm just someone . . ." He paused. " Someone to whom she meant a great deal."

" And where do I come in, I and my relatives ? "

He searched her face again with his steady look. " Her name means nothing to you ? "

" I'm afraid not."

" She was—is—about your age, but taller than you, very tall. Her hair's a reddish gold, a colour you'd remember if you'd seen it. Her eyes are a sort of golden-brown and her skin's very fair, with a lot of very small freckles . . ." He broke off. " No, you haven't seen her."

She shook her head, adding, " I'm sorry."

" Now please don't ask that other question you've just thought of," he said. " Have I been to the police ? Of course I have."

" The question I was actually going to ask," she said, " is the one I've already asked you—where do I and the Collivers come in ? "

He withdrew his eyes from her face, looking past her towards the door and in an amused tone, said, " There's poor Bertie, flapping his hands in an agony of impatience. We could talk again later, perhaps."

" Mr. Dreydel——"

" You see, I know I act outrageously," he said quietly. " One's apt to, when one's hard pressed."

" But why have you been asking questions about the Collivers ? Why are you suspicious of them ? "

His glance came back to her so swiftly and was so hard that it felt almost like a blow.

" Why are you ? " he asked

She stood up, feeling that he had set some trap for her and that she had stepped right into it.

" I think I will go and talk to Bertie," she said.

He stood up too. " Yes, I should. But you won't find he can tell you any more than I've told you myself."

" I think perhaps he may be able to," Helen said and walked away from him.

As she left the bar, she saw Bertie standing in the doorway of his office, staring hypnotically towards her as if he had been willing her to come to him. Seeing her, he made violent beckoning gestures with both hands.

Drawing her into the office and closing the door, he said, " I began to think you'd never come. I thought in there you understood me and after one or two minutes you'd follow me."

She laughed shortly. " That's what your friend said you thought. Now tell me what it's all about, Bertie. I find I tire very easily of mystery."

" First sit down, sit down," Bertie said, thrusting her towards a leather-covered armchair and holding out to her an enormous cigarette-case, filled with American cigarettes. " I only want to help, Miss Gamlen, not to interfere, not to stick my nose into anyone's private business. I don't like it when anyone sticks his nose into my business, and I don't stick my nose in anyone else's. Clear ? "

She gave a slight sigh, taking one of the cigarettes. " Absolutely clear."

" Very well now, listen." He perched on a corner of his large oak desk, agitatedly swinging one foot in the air. His square, pink face was full of earnest excitement. " Two weeks ago what happens ? Mr. Andras comes here. Young Andras. You remember him ? "

" Yes," Helen said, " I remember him."

" He comes here and he goes to see the Collivers. He comes back and he asks me, where's Mrs. Colliver ? I say, that's something nobody can tell you. He goes away and soon after this Dreydel turns up—Nicholas Dreydel, from Africa. And if I'm not wrong, Africa is a big place and it's very easy to say one comes from Africa. What do you think ? "

She nodded.

" So he comes here, this Dreydel, and he starts asking questions about Mrs. Colliver and Mr. Colliver and Miss Colliver. And again and again he looks through my register to see who's been staying here—oh, weeks, months, a year ago. And once he asked me what I knew about Mr. Colliver's other wives."

" *Wives !* " Helen said. She knew that Elvin Colliver had been a widower, but it had never occurred to her that her aunt had had more than one predecessor.

Bertie jumped off the desk and began to walk quickly up and down the small room, waving the hand that held the cigarette.

" And when you ask that man a question, he then asks you something else," he went on. " He asked me if I'd ever heard of a woman called Lillian Potter—Parker—Popper—some such name."

" Not Evelyn Lander ? "

" No, no," Bertie said, " it was Lillian—and Potter or Parker or Popper."

" Was she about my age, with red-gold hair and golden-brown eyes ? " Helen asked.

" No, she was a middle-aged lady with brown hair

turning a little grey . . ." He stood still. He looked at her queerly. "Why d'you ask me that, Miss Gamlen? D'you think you know such a person?"

"No, but Mr. Dreydel has been asking me about her. An Evelyn Lander with red-gold hair and golden-brown eyes and very tall."

"Maybe he's been doing some thinking then, since he spoke to me," Bertie said. "She sounds more interesting, eh, than this Mrs. Potter?"

"Then you don't believe in either of them?"

He flung up both hands. "I don't know what to believe. I only know, here comes Miss Gamlen herself now, who's not been here for a long time. First Mr. Andras, then Mr. Dreydel, then Miss Gamlen. And I think, it means something. It means someone is worried. It means Miss Gamlen is worried. And now I'll tell you again, I don't stick my nose into anybody's business but my own——"

"Yes, I know," Helen said, trying to mask her tension. "Go on, Bertie."

"Well then, it seems to me I should tell you about this man Dreydel and his questions," he said. "This I think all the more when he sees you and asks me questions about you. Then there's something else I think I should tell you. Your aunt—Mrs. Colliver . . ."

"Yes?"

"I'm only telling you the rumour there is here in Burnstone. I didn't start the rumour, I don't know where it did start. I only heard it. I heard it said that Mr. and Miss Colliver are great frauds, both of them, cheats, fakers. They rap with tables. They get messages from spirits. Myself I don't care what people do in such ways if it amuses them and if they can find fools to listen to them. But the rumour is that with all this rapping and writing and things flying through the air, they frightened poor Mrs. Colliver out of her mind and the reason no one can tell where she is, is that they've put her away in a lunatic asylum, so that they can have her house and her money to themselves!"

33

The last words had come out in a rush. He stopped now, rather red in the face and looking a little frightened.

Helen ground out her cigarette.

"What a horrible story—what a perfectly horrible story!"

Bertie nodded his head several times.

"But I think you can be fairly sure it isn't true," she said. "Mr. Colliver gave me my aunt's address. I shall go and see her next week-end and find out for myself how she is."

Bertie drew a deep breath. "Miss Gamlen, I *am* so glad to hear that. You know how it is with a rumour, no one believes it, everyone repeats it; then soon every-one believes it but gets too frightened to go on talking about it. And then it's really dangerous."

She nodded. "Yes, and as it happens, it isn't the only story I've heard. The other was quite as bad, though—well, I think even less probable."

"You're not angry then that I've repeated this ugly, foolish story to you?" he asked.

"I'm very grateful," she said. "But I'm very glad that I didn't hear it until after I'd seen the Collivers. In its horrible way, it fits the facts rather well. But as I said, Mr. Colliver gave me my aunt's address without any hesitation and seemed really pleased when I said I was going to see her. I don't think he'd have done that if either of these stories had been true."

"No," Bertie said thoughtfully. "No, that seems certain. But still . . ."

At something in his tone, exasperation flared in Helen. On the whole she liked life to be simple and a few days ago that was what it had been, a simple matter of dealing with the ordinary problems of work that she liked, of some not too complicated friendships, of some normal anxieties and everyday pleasures. But from the moment that she had looked into the eyes of Martin Andras, in the dark shadows of the staircase outside her door, that had all been spoilt.

"Well?" she said, trying to keep the exasperation out of her voice.

"This man Dreydel," Bertie said. "What are we to think about him?"

"Perhaps there's no need to think about him at all," she said. Then because of the look on Bertie's face, a dubious and faintly offended look, she added, "But thank you again, Bertie. It was good of you to tell me all this."

Before he could start it all over again, she left the office.

She went up to her room. As she climbed the stairs, she began to find herself almost wanting to champion the Collivers. Through their sheer unattractiveness and a few relatively harmless eccentricities, they seemed to inspire in everyone who met them suspicions that they had committed the direst crimes. And really, when you considered the matter, it was not fair of Aunt Violet to have allowed this to happen, not fair at all. After all, the man was her husband. She owed him something, even if, quite reasonably, she had decided that it was unbearable to live with him, his sister, their snake, their cats and their ghosts.

"Harmless eccentrics," Helen repeated to herself, taking off her tweed coat, throwing it on the bed and turning to the mirror. "And hasn't this always been the great country for them? We're proud of them. We breed them with care. If their supply failed, we'd feel that something had gone radically wrong with us. We'd begin to think there was nothing to distinguish us from Americans."

She liked the sound of that. Yet her own face, gazing back at her out of the mirror, was not quite satisfied.

V

HELEN SAW Nicholas Dreydel again at dinner. He was at a table in a corner of the room, which was fairly full, for people came to dine at the Old Swan from as far away as Oxford and Swindon.

Studying him when she could without his catching her at it, she thought that he looked like any normal, large, rather quiet man on holiday by himself and a little bored by his own company. But certainly that was not all that he was. He was a man with a mission of some kind. He was in Burnstone for a purpose. And the purpose was connected with Elvin Colliver and two women.

Or was there only one woman, whose name and appearance changed as the humour took him ? That is to say, was there really no woman at all ?

On her present supply of information, this was not a question to which Helen could venture any answer. So her mind moved on to other questions and to a decision, as a result of which, as soon as she had had dinner, she went upstairs to her room to fetch her coat.

Coming down and passing the dining-room door, she saw Nicholas Dreydel just getting up from his table. He saw her at the same time and hurriedly lifted a hand in a gesture that asked her to wait for him, but she went on quickly into the village street. She saw the look of frustration on his face, but he did not follow her. She walked in the same direction as she had taken earlier, but stopped before she reached the turning to Shipley's End and went in at the gate of a small white house, which was all over-grown, from the ground to its eaves, by an immense wistaria.

It was the letter from Mrs. Hindmarch, who lived here, to Martin's mother that had started all the trouble. Philip and Hannah Hindmarch were the kind of people who always write letters that start trouble, though they were a kind old couple, always the first people in the place to offer help in a time of sickness, arriving together to cook a meal, to take children to school or to put them to bed. Deeply united, they always went everywhere together, even to do the shopping for their frugal house-keeping or to post one of those dangerous letters, diffuse, evasive, not quite libellous, which, signed by one or the other, had always been jointly composed. Both were short, sturdy, white-haired and ruddy-faced, and looked so gentle and wholesome that it was amazing to discover

36

that their minds could entertain the suspicions they so dutifully sowed among their friends and neighbours.

When Helen rang their bell, it was Mrs. Hindmarch who opened the door to her, but her husband was only just behind her. At sight of Helen, both old faces lit up with pleasure and both voices exclaimed together that here was really a most extraordinary coincidence, because they had just been discussing whether or not they ought to write to her.

They took her into their small, neat, faded sitting-room, where she discovered that she would have to drink more tea. They asked her one or two routine questions about her health and her work, then they plunged, with solemn eagerness and with one earnest voice completing the unfinished sentences of the other, into a description of the scandalous negligence of the Collivers in maintaining Shipley's End.

It was some time before Helen had a chance of saying more than an occasional yes or no. But at last they returned to the strangeness of her appearing there at just the time when they had made up their minds that it was their duty to write to her to tell her that the fine old house was going to rack and ruin and that there were the most distressing rumours circulating about her aunt.

" But there's nothing strange about it," Helen managed to say. " I came because of your other letter, your letter to Mrs. Andras."

" To Mrs. Andras ? " they said together in startled voices. " Myra Andras ? "

" Yes," Helen said. " When she got it she sent Martin down here to look into things, then he came to see me. So that's why I came."

There was an unexpected hush in the small room. The Hindmarches looked at one another, then Philip Hindmarch said, " But we didn't . . ."

" No, of course we didn't . . ." his wife said.

" Write to Myra Andras," they said together.

" We should never have written to her, in any case . . ."

" . . . because we never, well . . ."

" . . . she isn't our type, you know."

37

" That isn't a criticism, of course, it's just . . . . . ."

" . . . just the way we happen to feel, I mean, that she isn't . . ."

" Sympathetic, if you know what we mean."

" So it would never have occurred to us to write to her . . ."

" . . . when we could write to you, dear."

" And that's what we were just discussing," they said together.

Half an hour later they were still saying the same thing and Helen could think of no reason for doubting them. They had never been in the least ashamed of their letter-writing or at all secretive about it. When a letter had been written, they spread the news of it far and wide. They described the struggles they had had with their consciences before undertaking it, and the calm they felt afterwards in knowing that a duty had not been shirked. Unhappily convinced that in truth they never had written to Martin's mother, Helen had to face the fact that the letter Mrs. Andras had received had been either a forgery or else a figment of Martin's imagination.

Walking back to the Old Swan, she thought mostly about the second of these possibilities. She even thought of telephoning to Martin from the hotel to charge him with it. But another thought chased this one away. Suddenly she thought of who might have forged the letter that had brought first Martin, then herself, to Burnstone. As soon as she reached the Swan, she went in search of him.

She found him in the bar, sitting by himself, reading, with a mug of beer on a low table in front of him. He stood up when he saw her, with the quick smile that only momentarily changed the gravity of his tanned face.

" I've been hoping you'd come," he said, " but I was afraid I'd frightened you away. What will you have to drink ? "

" Nothing, thanks." She sat down in a chair facing him. Her colour was higher than usual and her voice was nervous. " Mr. Dreydel, before dinner you told me that you'd been asking too many questions for an innocent traveller. Bertie confirmed that. You didn't tell me, however, and Bertie couldn't help me in this, why you'd been asking those questions. Are you going to tell me that now?"

"Do have a drink," he answered. "Please."

She shook her head.

He looked at her steadily. But she thought there was a slight change, a new wariness, in his expression.

After a moment he observed, "Something's happened, hasn't it?"

She nodded briefly.

"Do I get to know what it was?" he asked.

"At the moment," she answered, "I'm sticking to questions."

"Seems the habit's catching." He picked up his mug and drank from it. "As I remember it, I told you I was looking for someone. You told me you knew nothing about her. So that was that."

"You told Bertie you were looking for somebody else."

"No, strictly speaking, I didn't. I asked him if he'd every heard of a woman called Lillian Poplar and he said he hadn't. So that was that too. But I didn't tell him I was looking for her, because as it happens I know where she is."

"Where is that?"

"In a grave."

For an instant Helen did not believe that she had heard him correctly. Then a shudder shook her.

He went on. "I'm sorry, I didn't mean to shock you. But I've been living alone for a long time with some rather frightening thoughts."

"Because you're afraid that the other one—the one with the red-gold hair—is dead too?"

"Well . . ." He spoke slowly, sounding as if he were trying to say the least that he could. "It's a long time since I heard from her."

"But why come here to ask questions—and why questions about the Collivers and my aunt and me? And why write a letter to Mrs. Andras, signing it Hannah Hindmarch?"

" Wait a minute, wait a minute." He frowned at her across the top of his mug. " Would you say that again, please ? "

" Why did you write a letter to Mrs. Andras, who'll be the owner of Shipley's End when my aunt dies, telling her that it was going to rack and ruin and signing it Hannah Hindmarch ? "

" But I didn't," he said.

" I'm awfully inclined to think you did."

He thought that over for a moment, then remarked, " I seem to have created an unfortunate impression. Like most people, I've acted illegally in my day, but I honestly believe my crimes have been relatively minor ones. Forgery hasn't been among them."

It sounded convincing. But his face had turned oddly expressionless, as if he had deliberately arranged it so that it should reveal nothing contrary to what he was saying.

As Helen made no comment on it, he went on, " Tell me about this letter."

Helen shook her head. " Either you know about it already, or else there's no particular need for you to know. If I flung a false accusation at you, I'm sorry."

" But you don't think you did," he said.

" I don't know." She realised as she said it that her clear certainty of a few minutes ago that the forged letter had come from Nicholas Dreydel had somehow become blurred. It was not even clear to her just then why she had thought it. " I really don't know. But I've got an unpleasant feeling that someone or other is trying to manoeuvre me and a few other people into something— I don't know what and I don't know why—but it's something which requires that a fairly normal sort of situation should be made to seem fantastic and sinister." She stood up. " The one thing I know is that I don't like it."

She went to the door.

She had passed through it and reached the bottom of the staircase when she realised that Nicholas Dreydel had followed her.

Looking up at her as she started up the stairs, he said,
" Miss Gamlen, I didn't write that letter."

" Do you know who did ? " she asked.

" I didn't even know there'd been a letter," he said.

" Perhaps—perhaps there wasn't one, then," she said.
" Good night, Mr. Dreydel."

" Good night." He did not move, but remained there
looking up at her until she had passed the bend in the
staircase.

Helen spent a restless night, drifting in and out of
faintly nightmarish dreams and trying, in the troubled
intervals of waking, to make some sense of the discoveries
she had made the evening before. But mostly her con-
sciousness was possessed by the image of Martin Andras.
It was not that she thought about him, but simply that
he was there, vividly printed on her imagination, like a
photograph that has been accidentally superimposed on
another, distorting the other and making a slightly
frightening nonsense out of it.

All the love that she had ever felt for him at any time
helped to give his image a malign kind of charm, and
made her attempts to exorcise it only half-hearted. But
the confusion it caused at least helped her, as the hours
of the night passed, towards a resolution. This was that
she would say nothing whatever to Martin about the
letter, or indeed about her having come to Burnstone or
done anything at all as a result of his visit to her. She
would not telephone, she would not write, she would not
see him again. Then that bright, dark image would fade.

Next day she returned to London. Before she went she
had one more brief conversation concerning her aunt.
It was with an old friend, Dr. Pepall, and it came of a
chance meeting, while she was waiting for the bus to
take her back to Oxford. He was passing in his car,
recognised her and stopped.

He was a small, tousle-haired, untidy man, who
appeared as casual as he was in fact conscientious and as
fierce as he was really kind. Helen had experienced his
staunchness in her childhood.

He did not get out of his car when he saw her, but

41

barked questions at her through the window, overheard by the half-dozen other people who were waiting for the bus. After several questions about herself, he came to one about her aunt.

" Seen Mrs. Colliver lately, Helen ? "

" No," she answered, " but I'm hoping to next week-end."

" You know where she is, then ? "

" Yes, she's in Hampshire."

" Hampshire ? My God, why should anyone go to Hampshire ? "

" Why shouldn't she go to Hampshire ? "

" Might as well have stayed at home. Still, she's having a good rest, I suppose. Taking life easy for a change."

" I suppose so."

" That's good. Yes, I'm very glad to hear it. My God, how that woman used to work. Running that frightful old house almost single-handed and waiting on old Delborne hand and foot. Glad she got something out of it, at any rate, even if she hasn't had much chance to enjoy it. My God, what wouldn't I give for a housekeeper like that. But I haven't got the tyrant technique. Don't know how to turn people into willing slaves. . . . I suppose she *is* in Hampshire, Helen ? "

There it was again, the doubt, the suspicion, even in Dr. Pepall.

" I've got her address," Helen said.

" Good. Well, let me know how she is sometime. I like that old lady."

He gave her a wave and drove on, and a moment afterwards the bus arrived.

During the week that followed Helen was busy and as the everyday things of her life occupied her once more, some of the impressions of the week-end faded and she lost the sense of pressing anxiety about her aunt. With the address in Hampshire so readily given to her by Elvin Colliver, it seemed impossible that there could be anything serious the matter. The true explanation of her aunt's behaviour was, Helen believed, quite simple. She thought that

Aunt Violet, finding her marriage a grave disappointment, either because of the character of her husband or else because she had found that after all the married state did not really suit her, had quietly decided to cut her losses and clear out. She had done that, rather than persuade her husband and his sister to leave Shipley's End, probably for two reasons. One was the simple generosity of her nature, which would make it natural for her to deprive herself of the reward for her years of hard work for old Mr. Delborne, rather than act with the least ruthlessness or callousness to another person. The other reason was that almost certainly she hated to have to admit, face to face with the people she knew, the failure of her late, unexpected marriage.

That marriage had perhaps been a kind of triumph for her. She must have known that some people had laughed at it and that others, who were truly concerned for her, had had their forebodings, but at that time she had not cared. Not till later, when the happiness that she had expected had failed to develop, would she have started to shrink from the thought of her humiliation before her friends and gone quietly away without explanations.

All this seemed so certain to Helen that it barely needed corroboration. But she did not alter her intention of going down to the guesthouse at Burtonlea in Hampshire the next week-end. She had become uneasily conscious that for a long time she had neglected her aunt, who had shown her as much love as anyone she had ever known, so that it was, in any case, high time that she paid her a visit.

However, she did not telephone beforehand to warn her aunt that she was coming, and this was because some of the suspicion that Martin Andras, Nicholas Dreydel, Dr. Pepall and Bertie had sowed in her mind, had taken root there. For suppose that her aunt's voice, answering her, told her not to come, and suppose, just suppose for a moment, that that voice, sounding just like her aunt's, was in reality somebody else's . . .

VI

SHE WAS ridiculously relieved to see her aunt safe and sound.

She found her sitting in a sheltered corner of the garden of the guest-house at Burtonlea, a comfortable-looking, mid-Victorian house, set among orchards. Miss Colliver was wrapped up in a rug and wearing the old musquash coat that she had owned as long as Helen could remember.

At the sound of footsteps approaching across the lawn, Mrs. Colliver had looked up from her book and taken off her spectacles. But it must have been someone else whom she had expected to see, because, on recognising Helen, a delighted and astonished smile lit up her vague, gentle, brown eyes.

" Why, this is the very nicest thing that could ever have happened ! " she exclaimed, trying to disentangle herself from the rug and the deck-chair and to struggle to her feet.

Helen checked her with a hand on her shoulder and stooped to kiss her. There was a wooden bench nearby. Dragging it closer to Mrs. Colliver's chair, Helen sat down on it and looked critically at her aunt.

She was looking older and frailer than Helen had expected. Mrs. Colliver's skin had a new, dry, papery look that added years to her appearance, and her abundant, handsome, slatey grey hair had thinned and turned almost white. She had always stooped when she walked and in a chair had always huddled herself into the smallest space possible, but now she was looking smaller and more bowed than ever. There was least change in her big, shining, amiable, rather stupid, very dark eyes, and, of course, in her clothes. Not that the stolid grey felt hat that she was wearing was actually the same hat as that in which Helen had seen her last, but it was so indistinguishable from all the hats in which

Helen had ever seen her, that it seemed, like the fur coat, to be as old as Helen's memory. So did the mauve silk scarf that showed inside the collar of her coat, the broad-toed, low-heeled shoes and thick grey woollen stockings.

As Helen sat down, Mrs. Colliver laid a hand fondly on Helen's arm. The hand, which had once had a look of competence and strength, looked very fragile, emerging from the worn cuff of the old coat.

" Now tell me at once, dear, you've come for the week-end, haven't you ? You're not going to rush back to London to-day."

" I can stay if you'd like me to," Helen said. " D'you think I can have a room here ? "

" I'm sure you can, and it's very nice too," her aunt said. " I expect you can have the room Elvin always has when he comes. It's got such a pretty view towards the downs and on a clear day you can even see the sea. And you'll find the food's excellent. I'm enjoying that so much, you know—I mean, eating food I haven't cooked myself. Not that I don't feel sometimes that I could do better." She gave a little laugh and her hand, sliding down on to Helen's, tightened on it for a moment. " Dear, you can't think how happy I'm feeling, seeing you again. It was so good of you to come."

Responding to the pressure of her aunt's hand, Helen felt how loose the rings were on the thin fingers.

" And now tell me what this is all about," she said. " Tell me why you've gone into hiding."

Mrs. Colliver smiled as if Helen had said something very amusing.

" I wasn't very difficult to find, was I ? " she said.

" No, but a lot of people are very curious about where you are," Helen said. " It's a long time since you were last in Burnstone."

" I suppose it is, yes, a longish time," her aunt said.

" And you haven't written to any of your old friends."

" I wrote to you, didn't I ? "

" Only a postcard, which made me think you were just spending a holiday in Torquay."

" Why, so I was and it was very nice too—such a nice

45

hotel. I wish you could have come. My room had a lovely view across the bay and the food was excellent. And the weather was good, so sunny and nice. I really enjoyed myself."

"Aunt Violet," Helen said seriously, " don't dodge. Tell me what's happened."

Mrs. Colliver's dark eyes grew troubled. " But nothing's *happened*. What could have happened ? I don't understand you, dear."

" Tell me why you don't go home."

" Well, it's nice to have a change sometimes," Mrs. Colliver said. " Everyone likes that."

Helen nodded. She had realised already that she was going to need all her patience if she was to extract any information at all from her aunt. Mrs. Colliver was not a particularly intelligent woman, but she had long ago discovered the usefulness, whenever she felt herself on the defensive, of pretending to be even stupider than she was. By this simple method, she had routed Mr. Delborne again and again and kept him, in spite of his naturally overbearing temper and excellent intellect, in reasonable subjection. Suggestions concerning his household which she had not happened to welcome, criticisms, orders, demands, had all been quietly killed by her blank incomprehension.

" But your husband comes to see you here, does he ? " Helen asked. Her aunt's remark that she could probably have the same room as Elvin usually had when he came had startled her a good deal, yet this fact in itself, after all, would hardly have been startling at all, if she had not been influenced by the suspicions thrust into her mind by other people. She felt now that these were like a fog around her, concealing the true shapes of things.

" Why yes, he comes as often as he possibly can," Mrs. Colliver said, her soft, cow's eyes brightening. " He doesn't want me to be lonely—and I do get a little bit lonely sometimes, though the people here are very nice. Yes, very nice indeed, and we have some very interesting conversations at mealtimes. But when you've been used, as I have, for so many years, to the conversation of a gentleman like Mr. Delborne, you do notice that most other people aren't really intellectual. That's one of the reasons why I'm so glad when Elvin comes. He's a very intellectual man, very cultured and intellectual indeed. I always love to sit and hear him talk."

"Well, I'm glad he comes," Helen said. "I was afraid . . ."

"What, dear ? "

"Oh, that perhaps you weren't very happy with him and that that was why you didn't go home."

"Goodness me, why, he's the best man in the world ! " Mrs. Colliver exclaimed. "He's the kindest, most thoughtful man I've ever known. And so brilliant too, so well-informed and interesting. And Mignon's very clever too. In fact, she's a great deal more than clever, she's got a wonderful and extraordinary gift. She's very modest and quiet about it, but I daresay if you speak to her tactfully, she'll give you a demonstration of it sometime. But you do have to coax her a bit. She's very shy. Now let's go in and see about your room, shall we ? "

Helen decided to give up her questioning for the moment and reached out a hand to help her aunt from her chair.

The guest-house, as Mrs. Colliver had said, was quite comfortable. It was light and bright, in a chintzy way, with a great many highly polished brass ornaments and bowls of flowers. It was owned by two sisters who wore handwoven smocks and sandals, but the food, fortunately, was not of the wholemeal and raw vegetable type that this led Helen to fear. Lunch that day consisted of a creditable Hungarian goulash, followed by a moist, spongy sort of cake that tasted pleasantly of rum. Helen saw that her aunt ate well, indeed, almost greedily, as if, with little else to think about, food had become a major interest in her life.

After lunch, Mrs. Colliver said that she would lie down for a little and went up to her room. She reappeared in time for tea, and after tea suggested to Helen that they should go for a short walk. It was twilight outside and a wind had arisen, lifting up drifts of dead leaves and driving them through the air. In a few minutes' time Mrs. Colliver suggested turning back and she and Helen returned, to sit in a corner of the drawing-room. Mrs. Colliver took some knitting out of a bag and Helen started once more on her questioning.

" You know, Aunt Violet, you aren't looking too well," she said. " Is anything the matter ? "

" Only *anno domini*, dear," Mrs. Colliver answered placidly. " Nothing but nasty old *anno domini*."

" But what's it done to you ? " Helen asked, watching the small, bowed form in the chintz-covered armchair.

" Well, I'm just not so spry as I was," her aunt said. " But who'd expect it at my time of life ? "

" But the truth is, Aunt Violet, you aren't as old as all that," Helen said. " In fact, you're just putting on this age business. Come, why don't you tell me what's really the matter ? "

The knitting-needles clicked steadily.

" It's so kind of you to worry," Mrs. Colliver said, " but really and truly nothing's the matter."

" Then why have you left Burnstone without telling anyone where you were, so that the most dreadful rumours are circulating. Did you know that ? "

" Rumours, dear ? "

" Yes, Aunt Violet, rumours that Mr. Colliver has done something terrible to you so that he could get hold of the house and the money."

For the first time a look of distress appeared in the big liquid eyes, but the knitting-needles still clicked.

" Well, you know what it's like in a village," Mrs. Colliver said after a moment. " People will say just anything about a person they don't understand. I remember the things they used to say about Mr. Delborne when we first went there. He didn't spend all his time writing then, because he was a very active man when he was younger and he used to go about the country bird-watching and taking photographs, and so people started saying that he was a spy. They didn't say what country he was spying for, or what there was in Burnstone to spy on, because we hadn't got Hovard and Hayle's factory or even the steam laundry yet, but still they said he was a spy. Then they got used to him slowly and became very proud of having such a clever, intellectual man living in their midst. And you'll see, they'll get used to Elvin bit by bit, and realise that it's really a privilege to have someone like him in the village."

"Not if he lets the house and garden go to pieces, as he's done so far," Helen said.

She had hoped that this would rouse her aunt in some way. Shipley's End had been very dear to her and a great source of pride. That she could have become quite indifferent to its condition seemed impossible.

Mrs. Colliver gave a slight sigh and for a moment the knitting was lowered into her lap and her hands lay still.

"I'm afraid Mignon isn't a very good manager," she said, "and Elvin doesn't know anything about gardens. One can't know everything and with their talents . . ." The knitting-needles were moving again. "But I'll admit, dear, though I wouldn't to anyone but you, that I do worry, and if Mr. Delborne himself hadn't said . . ." She stopped suddenly with a strange look of fear on her face.

"What did Mr. Delborne say?" Helen asked.

"Oh dear!" Mrs Colliver exclaimed as the ball of wool in her lap fell to the floor and shot away under tables and chairs. "Oh dear, how clumsy of me! Would you be very sweet and get it back for me, Helen?"

Helen retrieved the ball of wool. It took her a little while, apologising to the various old ladies and gentlemen who were sitting in the chairs, as she rolled the ball back beneath them.

Sitting down again, she said, "Now, Aunt Violet, what did Mr. Delborne say?"

Mrs. Colliver's face was quite calm again.

"I didn't mean Mr. Delborne," she said. "That was a slip of the tongue, because I was thinking about him. I meant to say Mr. Colliver."

"Then what did Mr. Colliver say?"

"He said . . . Slip one, knit two together, purl two. . . . Really I forget what I was going to say about him, dear. So silly of me. But I keep doing that nowadays. I start to say something and then I quite forget what it was. Now just wait a moment while I count my stitches."

By now Helen was deeply worried. That incautious reference to Mr. Delborne, followed by the look of fear, was something that she could not forget. But she realised that there was no chance of outwitting a cunning as blatant and laborious as her aunt's, and that for the time being further questioning was useless.

As the evening passed, Helen thought she saw that look of fear again, or if it was not actually of fear, at least it was a look both sly and desperate, very strange and very perturbing in Mrs. Colliver's innocent eyes. Talking of other things, Helen's feeling that it was of the greatest importance to induce her aunt to confide in her grew more and more urgent, yet the knowledge that every approach she made, direct or indirect, would be baulked by the same obvious little tricks and evasions made her presence seem irritatingly futile. She went early to bed. It was only after she had reached her room and half-undressed that she remembered that there was one question that she might have asked which just conceivably might have startled her aunt into some helpful self-betrayal.

Helen saved up this question until the afternoon of the following day, when she was saying good-bye to Mrs. Colliver. As the time when Helen must leave to catch her train had come closer, Mrs. Colliver had grown restless and even vaguer and more muddled in her speech than before. But Helen had the feeling that the vagueness now was genuine and not assumed to defend some secret. She thought that her aunt was really distraught, and showing for the first time signs of a great unhappiness.

"Helen, dear . . ." Mrs. Colliver caught suddenly at her hand and twined her fingers tightly through Helen's. "You will come again, won't you? You'll come and see me again soon?"

They were standing by the open door and a shaft of pale sunshine fell directly on Mrs. Colliver's face. It looked like a haggard child's face, lost and scared. She thrust it closer to Helen's.

"Please," Mrs. Colliver said in an unsteady whisper. Helen laid her cheek against her aunt's.

"Of course, if you want me to."

"I've wanted you so much, for so long, but Mr. Delborne . . . No, I don't mean that, but I keep thinking about him, you know, and so his name slips out. He was such a wonderful man, wasn't he? But perhaps you don't really remember. I spent thirty years of my life looking after him, and I'd always do anything he wanted. . . . Helen, dear, you will come and see me soon, won't you?"

"I'll come next week-end, if you like," Helen said.

"Will you really? Oh, but you're so busy, you've so many friends, you won't want to bother with me. Truly I don't want to bother you. And Elvin does come as often as ever he can, so I'm not really lonely. But will you really come next week-end?"

"Yes, for sure," Helen said. "But there's something I've just remembered, Aunt Violet. When I was in Burnstone last week-end, Miss Colliver made me promise to ask you something. I don't understand the question at all, but perhaps you will."

Mrs. Colliver gave a sudden bright smile. "Mignon wanted you to ask me something?" she said eagerly.

The smile and the eagerness surprised Helen.

"Yes, she wanted to know if Mr. Delborne used to keep a spare pair of spectacles and a small red book in the drawer of the table beside his bed."

"Yes—yes, he did!" Mrs. Colliver said excitedly. "Isn't that extraordinary. She really has a gift, you know—a wonderful gift. Because she couldn't possibly have known that by herself. I shouldn't think anyone knew it except me and I know I never told her."

Her face, which a moment before had looked so haggard and empty, was full of life.

"I see," Helen said thoughtfully. "Yes, I think

perhaps I begin to see . . . something. Good-bye then, till next Saturday."

" It's a wonderful gift," Mrs. Colliver repeated, as if she had not heard Helen speak. " I don't envy her for it, because the strain of it is often terrible. I'm sure I could never bear it. But I think it's wonderful."

" Yes, wonderful." Helen kissed her aunt and started for the station. She was not sure that her aunt, standing in the doorway, rapt and excited, even noticed her go.

" Wonderful, wonderful ! " Helen muttered furiously as she hurried along. " My God, yes, it's wonderful ! " She was as angry as she had ever been in her life.

VII

As soon as she reached her flat in London she telephoned Martin.

His voice, answering her, was surprised and in some way cautious.

" Helen ? It's really Helen ? "

" Yes, and I want to talk to you," she said. " When can you come here ? "

" Now," he said.

" I was hoping for that. Martin . . ."

" Yes ? "

" I went to Burnstone a week ago and this week-end I've been to a place in Hampshire where Aunt Violet's staying."

" Did you see her ? " he asked quickly.

" Yes."

" Is she all right ? "

" That's what I want to discuss with you. There's something wrong, but I know only a little about it. I can make a few guesses of a rather horrible kind, but I don't know how to go on from there."

" But she's alive ? You did see her ? "

" Oh yes, she's alive."

" Thank God for that! "

He said it with such fervour that Helen was startled. She had not thought that he cared so much about her aunt.

" Then I'll expect you in half an hour or so," she said.

" I'm on my way," he answered.

She had telephoned him before even taking off her coat or lighting the gas fire. Now, putting down the telephone, she looked round the room and saw that the flowers that had been fresh enough the day before were beginning to fade, and that there was a film of dust on the furniture. Lighting the fire, she picked up the vase of flowers and carried it out to the kitchen, came back with a duster and went rapidly round the room, setting it to rights.

After that she went into her bedroom, took off her coat and changed her dress. It was only when she was fastening the clasp of a necklace that she met her own eyes in the mirror. As they looked back at her, their gaze grew sardonic. Suddenly her fingers fumbled with the clasp, as if she had just become unsure whether or not she wanted to wear the necklace. For a moment she felt the same sensation of fright that she had felt when she had seen Martin on the stairs, about ten days before. She knew that since that evening her feelings had been in a state of confusion and that she might have been far wiser to have stuck to her resolution not to see him again. But something imperative had driven her to the telephone. It had seemed reasonable, even necessary, to discuss the situation at Burnstone with Martin, who had first made her aware of it, and who in some ways was as much concerned in it as she was herself. Yet, as she hesitated, looking into her own eyes, she knew that her motive in asking him to come to see her had been by no means so simple.

At that moment the bell rang. Shrugging her shoulders, she fastened the clasp of the necklace, hurriedly screwed ear-rings on to her ears and went to the door.

When she opened it he was standing just outside it. From the look on his face and from a movement he made, she thought that he was going to take her in his arms. Then she saw that the movement had not been towards her, but merely towards the door, so that he could thrust it farther open. As he did so, he stepped to one side and Helen saw that he was not alone. From behind him, having climbed the stairs more slowly than he, came a small, dark, elegant woman.

Walking into the room ahead of Martin, she gave Helen a cool smile and in a light, sweet voice, said, " Hallo, Helen—I thought you wouldn't mind if I came too."

Helen's momentary confusion turned instantly into a quiet rage. It was not that, if she had been prepared for it, she would have objected to the presence of Myra Andras, but recognising in the insincere smile and the charming, empty voice, all the old antagonism that Martin's mother had always felt for her, she thought furiously that Martin had had no right to inflict this upon her just now, of all times. He knew of the feelings in his mother as well as Helen did herself, and should somehow, she thought, have prevented this happening, or at least given warning of it.

Myra Andras walked to the middle of the room, looked round it deliberately, then as carefully looked Helen up and down.

" How well you look," she said, " and how lovely."

But she was a more beautiful woman herself, even at fifty, than Helen could ever be. She was slenderer, more delicately made, with a look at all times of fragile yet consciously powerful femininity. Or so Helen felt, suspecting at the same time that Myra's compliment was merely to be a reminder of this.

Usually suspicions of this sort did not play an abnormally strong part in Helen's character, but Myra Andras had always had the knack of bringing all the worst in her to the surface. Because of this, Helen always became tongue-tied in her presence, losing all her self-confidence and feeling herself thrust back almost into the clumsiness of adolescence.

" Quite lovely," Myra said. " It's so long since I've

seen you, I'd forgotten that. And what a charming room. It looks as it you're very prosperous." She walked towards the fire, loosening the short, black, broadtail jacket that she was wearing over a simple, perfectly cut black dress. " I wish I were prosperous," she said.

Helen looked questioningly at Martin. But he kept his eyes expressionlessly on his mother, as if this provided him with some sort of defence against the antagonism between the two women.

Myra went on, " I suppose you think that's why I've been worrying about Miss Gamlen, Helen."

Martin corrected her, " Mrs. Colliver."

" Oh yes—I find it so difficult to remember that she's married," Myra said with a bright smile. " Well, Helen—don't you ? "

" Don't I what ? " Helen said.

" Don't you think my worrying about your aunt must be from rather interested motives ? "

" Why, I've been assuming you were worrying in a quite normal way," Helen said.

" You have ? How nice of you. Isn't it nice of her, Martin, to give me the benefit of the doubt, instead of jumping to the conclusion that I was only worrying about the house and the money ? "

Martin's dark brows twitched, but he said nothing.

Helen said irritably, " If the thought of the house and the money hadn't crossed your mind, you wouldn't be human, but I don't suppose you've been actively wishing for my aunt's death." Very ungraciously, she added, " Will you have some sherry ? "

" Thank you, yes, that's just what I should like." Myra drew off her gloves, holding out a hand, with a flash of rings, to the fire. " I can't afford sherry. At least, only South African."

" This is South African," Helen said grimly.

" Ah well, it's excellent. Really one can hardly tell the difference." But somehow the way she said it only emphasised the fact that the difference was enormous. " Now tell us about Miss Gamlen, Helen. You told Martin you'd seen her."

" Yes." Helen filled three glasses and brought them across the room. " Martin's fear that she'd been murdered by her husband and buried in the garden turned out to be unfounded."

" Martin ! " His mother turned on him in astonishment. " Did you really tell Helen an unspeakable thing like that ? "

" It was your own idea, wasn't it ? " he said.

" Certainly not. I only said . . . Well, never mind. At any rate, I never dreamt that you'd . . . But go on, Helen. Tell us what's really happened to the poor old thing."

" The trouble is, I don't know," Helen said. " I went to Burnstone last week-end and put up at the Swan for the night. I went to see the Collivers and I found both of them and the state of the house quite as depressing as Martin had told me. I found that Miss Colliver goes in for second sight or extra-sensory perception or something, and I discovered from Bertie at the Swan that there was a nasty rumour around that the Collivers had used this somehow to scare my aunt out of her wits, so that they could put her away in a lunatic asylum and have the house and her income for themselves."

" But that's perfectly horrible ! " Myra Andras said sharply, in a tone which even Helen was ready to admit sounded perfectly sincere.

" Yes—because it almost might be true," she said, " whereas the idea of murder wasn't quite convincing."

Martin observed, " Yet murders happen."

" But Aunt Violet's much more useful to the Collivers alive than dead," Helen said. " Dead, all her assets come to you. And they gave me her address without the slightest reluctance and seemed to be genuinely glad when I said I was going to see her. That made me think that the obvious explanation must be the true one. That's to say, that Aunt Violet had decided her marriage had been a mistake and just deserted her husband. And because she's the sort of person who's never stood up for herself in her life and always blamed herself rather than anyone else for anything that's gone wrong, she'd naturally not have thought of turning the Collivers out of the house, but would have gone away herself."

Myra nodded. "That's what I told Martin myself. I said I was sure that was the true explanation. Didn't I, Martin?"

"Yes," Martin said. "I think among other things you said that."

"Yet it isn't the true explanation," she said. "Helen doesn't think so any longer—do you?"

"I don't know, it may be," Helen said. "But at least it isn't the whole explanation. You see, that same evening, I found . . ." She hesitated, discovering only then and without knowing why, that she had no intention of mentioning the man called Nicholas Dreydel. "I found out," she went on, "that the letter you got from Mrs. Hindmarch hadn't been written by her at all."

As she said this, she looked quickly from Myra's face to Martin's, not sure what expression she expected to catch on one or the other. But the expressions on both faces were merely puzzled and a little incredulous.

"Have you still got that letter?" Helen asked.

"Yes, at home," Myra said. "How do you know it didn't come from the Hindmarches?"

"Simply that they said it didn't," Helen said.

"Good enough, I suppose. But all the same, I don't think there's anything very mysterious about the letter. It was probably written by some other busybody in Burnstone, who wanted to stay anonymous, as such people often do, and so signed it Hindmarch."

"That could be so," Helen agreed.

Almost for the first time since he had entered the room, Martin's eyes met hers directly. He gave her a tight-lipped smile.

"Only you don't think so, do you?" he said in a mocking voice.

Myra shrugged. "It doesn't matter. Go on about Miss Gamlen, Helen. You've actually seen her?"

Helen noticed how she harped on this question, almost as if she doubted Helen's statement.

"Yes, I spent most of yesterday and to-day with her,"

Helen said. " She's staying at a quite pleasant guest-house at a place called Burtonlea. She's looking much older than when I saw her last, and not too well, and she seems to be rather lonely and unhappy. But she seems to adore her husband and he keeps visiting her at the guest-house. I was quite wrong about the marriage having broken up."

" Then what's worrying you ? " Myra asked.

" Two things," Helen said. " One is that she mentioned Mr. Delborne several times, as if—well, as if he'd given her instructions of some sort, which she was trying to carry out. And the mere thought of them or of him, seemed to terrify her. I think that was the most worrying part of it all, that she was so scared about something."

" But that's absurd," Myra said. " Instructions ! He left her the house and a good income and unless he left her instructions to enjoy them for as long as possible, so that I shouldn't get them, I'm sure he left her no instructions at all. And I hope she appreciates the fact that I made no efforts to break that will. I didn't because I thought she'd had a dog's life for thirty years and that she deserved some return, but I shouldn't be surprised if in fact I could have broken it quite easily."

In a voice that had suddenly grown tense with the suppression of some violent feeling, Martin said, " What's the other thing that's worrying you, Helen ? "

She gestured uncertainly. " Well, I think the Collivers are playing some awful trick on her, exploiting her somehow or other. She's extremely credulous and easily impressed, and she thinks Miss Colliver's ' gift,' as they all call it, is simply wonderful. I think—no, I don't know what I think exactly, except that they've worked on her somehow with their spiritualism to stay away from the house."

" Well, that's her own fault and nothing for us to worry about," Myra said. " At least she's alive, reasonably well and living in comfort. Personally I wish I could afford a spell in hotels and guest-houses as a change from the daily grind." She spoke impatiently and with some other feeling in her voice that Helen could not identify. Was it merely disappointment? Picking up her gloves and drawing her fur jacket around her once more, Myra added, " It's been nice seeing you, Helen. I'm sorry if our false alarms about Miss Gamlen worried you. To me it's obvious that she's just taken to living as she's wanted to all her life, with her husband's odd beliefs adding a pleasant spice to things. And really I don't blame her at all." She went towards the door. " Why don't you ring me up some time? We'll go to a theatre."

She was all at once in a hurry to be gone, giving Helen another of her cool, distant smiles. Martin went with her. After a moment Helen heard their car start under her window and drive away.

For a little while she stood in the middle of the room, looking vaguely around her. A frown gathered on her forehead. Absently she fingered the necklace round her neck. Then she fetched the bottle of South African sherry, and, glad to see that the bottle was still half full, refilled her glass and started to drink it.

There was a knock at the door.

When she opened it, she found Martin there again.

" But I heard you drive away," Helen asserted, as if to disprove his presence.

" No, she went by herself," he said.

" Well, come in, then."

" No," he said. " I came back just to tell you something."

" Well? "

" I couldn't help her coming," he said. " She was there when you telephoned. But don't get her wrong, Helen. She isn't greedy. She was really worried about your aunt."

" I hope so," Helen said.

" I was worried too."

She did not answer.

" I was," he said, " and I'm glad to know that she's alive. *You don't know just how damn' glad I am!* "

He turned quickly and ran down the stairs.

Closing the door again, Helen went slowly back to the

fire. She picked up her glass of sherry and sipped it slowly. She was quite sure that Martin had just spoken the truth. But because of the way that he had spoken, the words exploding out of him with an emotion that she could not at all understand, she was suddenly even more distraught than before.

"But that's all nonsense," she said aloud. "Of course he's glad and why shouldn't he say so?"

Going into the kitchen, she started to cook herself some bacon and eggs.

At intervals during the evening she repeated that there was nothing to worry about, and as she argued the case with herself, found herself presently almost repeating what Myra Andras had said, that Aunt Violet was probably thoroughly enjoying a leisurely life in one hotel after another, and that if in some way she was being exploited by the Collivers, she was a more than willing victim.

From that point Helen argued herself into making the assertion that she was not her aunt's keeper, and almost persuaded herself to go back on her promise to visit her again next week-end.

However, on the following Saturday, she returned to the Etherfield Guest-house. There she was told by the two home-spun sisters that only two days after her former visit, Mrs. Colliver had suddenly packed up and gone away. She had left a forwarding address—Shipley's End, Burnstone.

VIII

IN THE train on her way back to London, Helen felt puzzled, angry and as if someone, she did not know who, or for what conceivable purpose, had succeeded in making a fool of her. But she had had enough of it. She had a job to think about and not unlimited time or money to waste on the eccentricities of a relation whose professed desire to see her was certainly not sincere.

Yet next morning saw Helen again at Paddington, buying a ticket to Oxford.

She was still in a bad temper. But during the night she had discovered that her sense of responsibility, roused by the unfamiliar look of feebleness and the unexplained fear that she had seen in her aunt's great, gentle eyes, was not going to let her rest. She would have to do something about it. She would have to make at least one more effort to arrive at some explanation of Mrs. Colliver's troublesome behaviour.

This time she did not take a bag with her. She had no intention of staying the night. By starting out early, she thought, she could reach Burnstone by midday, cope with the Collivers before lunch and catch a train back to London in the afternoon.

But things did not work out as simply as that.

First, she had forgotten that on a Sunday no buses ran from Oxford to Burnstone until after one o'clock. So, unless she was prepared to have her plans upset and spend two hours wandering about Oxford on a day which had turned out cold, rainy and depressing, she had no alternative but to take a taxi. But this was so expensive that when she had paid for it, she found that she had just sevenpence halfpenny left in her purse, which was not even enough to pay her bus-fare back to Oxford. This meant that she would either have to borrow some money from the Collivers, which was an expedient that she did not even consider, or ask Bertie to cash a cheque. Though she had no qualms about doing this, it helped to make her feel that everything that day was bound to go wrong. Then, going into the Old Swan to look for Bertie she came face to face with Myra Andras.

The meeting appeared to be as much of a shock to Myra as it was to Helen. Her face went rigid and she quite forgot to produce one of her remote smiles.

Then, in a tone which was like an accusation of unspeakable things, she said, " Why, it's Helen ! "

Feeling the speechlessness coming on that was always likely to afflict her when she met Myra, Helen nodded impatiently and looked round her, hoping to see Bertie.

Myra, noticing the look, said, " Martin isn't here. I'm by myself."

That, Helen felt, was something to be thankful for. The meeting the week before had vividly reminded her of how much she had always disliked seeing Martin in Myra's company.

" Well, since you're here," Myra went on, " come and have a drink."

There was a marked lack of warmth in the invitation but she started walking towards the bar, which had just been opened, as if she assumed that Helen would follow her.

Helen thought of having to explain, when it came to her turn to buy a drink for Myra, that she had only sevenpence halfpenny in her bag.

" If you don't mind," she said, " I'd like to see Bertie first."

But Myra was already pushing open the swing-doors and appeared not to hear her. In a worse temper than ever, Helen followed her and found herself being asked what she would have to drink, not by Myra, but by a stout, white-haired man who called Myra " my dear " and who, as soon as she had come close enough, had captured one of her hands in his and held on to it.

Myra introduced him to Helen as Mr. Hovard.

He said cheerily, " But if you're going to ask me if I'm Hovard of Hovard and Hayle, Miss Gamlen, the answer is no, I'm no one so exalted, though my line isn't really so different from theirs. But the name is entirely a coincidence. Now what are you going to drink? Try one of their martinis—they don't make them badly here, or so I'm told. I always stick to straight gin myself."

He had a loud, confident voice and spoke with a wide smile, showing excellent teeth. He was of medium height, looking big beside Myra, and was probably about fifty, though if there had been less flesh on him he might have looked younger. The skin of his plump, blunt-featured face was pink and unlined, and though his hair was white, his bushy eyebrows were still dark. He wore checked tweeds, a yellow pullover and a yellow tie with a pattern of horses on it.

"And Myra," he said, "little Myra—I know she'll have a martini, eh, my dear?"

He swung her captured hand backwards and forwards inside his own large, pink fist. Myra surprisingly blushed a little.

"Lovely little Myra," he said. "Two martinis, John, and a straight gin. You know, Miss Gamlen, this little lady's quite wonderful. She's got a great big grown-up son. You'd never believe it, would you?"

"Miss Gamlen and my son are acquainted," Myra said. "You can stop laying it on, Harold."

"I never lay it on," he said. "I speak straight from my heart. That's why I keep my cheerful, uncomplicated view of life. Wait now . . ." He reached out suddenly and drew towards him a vase filled with michaelmas daisies that stood at one end of the counter. Breaking off a small spray of the flowers, he threaded it through a buttonhole of the black suit that Myra was wearing. His great pink hands seemed to stray all over her while he was doing it. "Not an orchid," he said, "not even a camellia, but still it's a lovely little flower for a lovely little woman—and d'you know something, Miss Gamlen, it means more to me than orchids and camellias? And d'you know why? It's because there were these things, whatever they're called, in this very same vase, the first time I ever saw her. Here she was, sitting in the corner here at this bar, with these purple thingummies making a halo behind her lovely dark head——"

"For God's sake!" Myra interrupted. But she did not remove the little daisies from her buttonhole and she had not shrunk from his hands when he was putting them there.

"I swear it's true," he said solemnly. "I'll always remember them."

"Don't listen to him, Helen," Myra said. "He makes it all up as he goes along. You've come looking for Miss Gamlen, I suppose, but you could have saved yourself the trouble. She isn't here. Or—*haven't* you come looking for her ? "

Helen turned this question over in her mind before she answered it, then she said, " So you know she isn't at Burtonlea any more."

" If she ever was there," Myra said.

" I don't understand you," Helen said. " I saw her there."

" So you told me before. But I didn't see her there myself."

" That sounds," Helen said thoughtfully, " as if you were trying to say something extraordinarily nasty."

" I'm just getting down to brass tacks," Myra said. " Like Harold, I'm speaking straight from my heart. I think something remarkably fishy is going on and I'm not quite convinced that you aren't mixed up in it."

" My dears, my dears," Harold Hovard said, " drink up your martinis, remember you're two good little girls and be kind to one another."

" If I'm wrong," Myra added, " I'll apologise."

" Big of you," Helen muttered. She was trying to resist the numbing effect that Myra always had on her, but at the same time she realised that if she were not careful, her temper, already on edge, would get out of hand. Taking Harold Hovard's advice, she sipped her martini and thought carefully before she spoke.

Myra took the opportunity to say, " I went down to Burtonlea myself last week. That was on Wednesday. And I was told Miss Gamlen had left on Tuesday."

" But then you know she *had* been staying there," Helen said.

" I know someone had been staying there," Myra answered. " Someone calling herself Miss Gamlen—I mean, Mrs. Colliver. And I know someone calling herself Mrs. Colliver stayed at that hotel in Torquay. But it strikes me as odd that as soon as Martin or I take an interest in this person, she disappears."

" Meaning," Helen said, trying to keep her voice level, " that since she doesn't disappear when I go to see her and as I know she isn't Aunt Violet, I must be in a conspiracy with her and the Collivers to defraud you out of your house and your money. Isn't that it? You're still sticking to the idea that Aunt Violet's dead and the house and the money are really yours. Spoken in front of a witness, that sounds to me uncommonly like slander."

To her surprise, she saw that Myra looked nervous.

" Don't be silly, Helen, of course I don't mean anything like that," she said. " All the same, I do think something very fishy is going on. You must admit that your aunt isn't behaving in the least like her usual self."

" Oh, I admit that," Helen said.

" And that I've a right to know . . ." Myra's voice faltered. " Oh, never mind. Let's talk about something else."

" That's right, and have another drink on the good resolution," Harold Hovard said jovially.

" But I may as well tell you," Myra went on, taking no notice of him, " that I've been up to the house and seen those unspeakable people and they were by no means so willing to give me your aunt's new address as you say they were to give you her old one. In fact, I was pretty tartly told to mind my own business."

" Another drink ! " Harold Hovard repeated. " You both look so solemn, one'd think this old lady you're talking about had just disinherited the two of you."

" She can't do that," Myra said with a tight-lipped smile. " Can she, Helen ? "

Helen put down her glass so that it clanged on the counter. She turned quickly and went out. Her face felt so hot that she thought it must be crimson, but catching sight of herself in a mirror in the lobby, she found that she was in fact more than usually pale. She went to the door of Bertie's office and drummed a furious tattoo upon it, stopping in confusion when he jerked the door open and thrust out a startled face.

" Oh dear, I'm sorry," she said. " I was thinking about something else."

" I'm glad," Bertie said sombrely. " When you think about me, please never look like that. What can I do for you ? "

She told him her predicament and asked if he would cash a cheque for three pounds.

He agreed and she went into the office, sitting down at his desk to write, while he took three pound notes out of his wallet and handed them to her. His face remained serious and his manner was more formal than usual. He asked her if she wanted to stay the night and when she replied that she would be returning to London, she thought that he looked relieved.

" I don't expect so many people to stay at this time of year," he said. " When the summer season ends, I let half the staff go. But now with Mr. Dreydel and Mr. Hovard and Mrs. Andras . . ." He gestured helplessly.

" So Mr. Dreydel's still here," Helen said.

" Oh yes, it looks as if he's going to stay for ever."

" And still asking questions ? "

" All the time. And Mr. Hovard too."

" He asks questions ? "

He nodded. " I don't like it, Miss Gamlen. It makes me nervous. I'm so nervous I keep expecting something terrible to happen. That's why I jumped like I did when you started to beat the door down. It's happened now, I thought. God knows what it is, but it's happened. That's the police."

" I'm really sorry," she said. " What does Mr. Hovard ask questions about ? "

" About Shipley's End. He's been here several times, always asking questions about it. I think he wants to buy it."

" Surely not. It doesn't look his sort of place at all."

" I think he does, though."

" Unless, of course . . .." An idea had just struck her and she puzzled over it for a moment. " Bertie, d'you think it's true that he's nothing to do with Hovard and Hayle ? "

" I believe so," Bertie said. " Young Mr. Hayle comes in here sometimes and I asked him once. He was angry about it. He said this Hovard is a manufacturer of quack medicines and nothing at all to do with their Mr. Hovard."

" Because if he were connected with them . . . But they're decent people, aren't they ? They wouldn't get up to anything tricky about buying property hereabouts. Besides, why should they want Shipley's End ? "

" I don't know," Bertie said. " But I'm tired of questions. They make me nervous. And still the shocking stories about poor Mrs. Colliver. You haven't seen her, I suppose, Miss Gamlen ? "

" Oh yes, I saw her."

He looked astonished. To Helen, in her highly strung mood, it also seemed for a moment that he looked disbelieving, but he only said, " Good, good, that's very good news. Aren't people terrible, the things they'll say ? Believe me, in my job, I see the worst of human nature. Terrible ! "

" Terrible," Helen agreed, getting up to go. She would have found it impossible just then to mention the fact that although she had seen her aunt, Mrs. Colliver had disappeared again.

She went out into the thin, cold rain that was still falling. The village street was empty and looked depressing and almost squalid under a leaden sky. The road was slimy and the ditches were full of muddy water. Helen hurried, slithering occasionally on sodden leaves trodden flat to the ground. Reaching Shipley's End, she swung the gate open and was starting up the drive to the door when an amazing sight caught her eye and she stood still, staring.

Elvin Colliver, wearing wellington boots and a duffle coat with the hood up over his head, was patiently, steadily digging in the garden. He was working on one of the rose-beds, forking out all the weeds and throwing them on to a pile nearby. He worked slowly, puffing a good deal, but keeping on stubbornly.

After she had watched him for a moment, Helen picked her way towards him across the long, wet grass.

" Rather wet for gardening, isn t it ? " she said.

He started violently. Straightening up, he clapped a hand to the small of his back and rubbed it.

" My dear Helen—I didn't hear you come," he said.

"Yes, it is rather wet, yet I like it, I find. It exhilarates me. Or do you mean that it's a mistake to dig when the ground's so wet? I've wondered about that—whether one ought to walk on it at all, I mean. I know so little about gardening that I sometimes think I'm likely to do as much harm as good. What do you think?"

"I don't know anything about it either," Helen said.

He went on rubbing his back. "I began on it the day after your last visit. It started me thinking, you know. I realised how neglected the place must have looked to you and that if I didn't tackle it soon, it would get completely out of hand. So I made a resolution that I'd dig for an hour a day, wet or fine. And really I think it's made a difference already. But you mustn't stand there in the rain. Come inside and let's see what Mignon can do in the way of lunch."

Leaving the fork stuck into the rose-bed, he walked stiffly towards the house.

Mignon had seen them talking in the garden and was waiting in the doorway to greet Helen. She was wearing the same stained purple dress as before, but the large grey Persian cat that she held clasped in her arms was one that Helen had not yet seen. So was the slim black cat that was rubbing itself against Mignon's ankles.

In a hurried, earnest murmur, Mignon said, "This is very fortunate. I was going to write to you, but now we can talk, which is so much more satisfactory. You did go to see Violet, didn't you? You did see her?"

Her brother said, "Now let the poor girl at least get inside the house before you start talking. It's raining, you know." He pushed back his hood and started fumbling with the fastenings of his duffle coat. "Come in," he said heartily to Helen, "come in and get warm. I'm sorry I can't offer you a drink, because Mignon and I never touch alcohol. Mignon found it definitely harmed her powers of concentration. But I'm sure we can manage something nice and warming for lunch in the way of stew—eh, Mignon? We didn't finish the Irish stew last night, did we?"

"No," Mignon said absently, "I don't think so. Yes,

come in, Helen. The fire isn't going very well yet, the wood was so wet, but I expect it'll burn up presently."

She turned and scuttled into the drawing-room.

If possible, it looked even dirtier and untidier than it had the week before and the fire was even smaller and more discouraging. Helen said that she would keep on her coat and declined firmly to stay for lunch. She looked cautiously round the room for stray snakes and Mignon, seeing this, observed that the lovely creature was in its box in her bedroom.

"You don't like snakes, I'm afraid," she said wonderingly. "The cats don't either. But now I want you to tell me about Violet. Did you ask her that question— the one about the red book and the spectacles?"

"Now wait, now wait," Elvin said. "Let's ask her first if she can tell us where Violet is."

Helen, who had just been making certain that something she saw in front of her feet was in truth only a wrinkle in the rug and not any kind of tame serpent, looked at him quickly. He was wiping the raindrops off his face with a soiled handkerchief.

"Then you don't know where she is?" she asked.

"Well, we know she's in Blackpool, but we don't know her address there," he said.

"*Blackpool!*"

"Yes, she sent us a picture-postcard." He went to a table that was thickly piled with papers of all kinds, including what looked like some grease-proof paper that had at some time wrapped a pound of butter. "It's somewhere here, I think."

"But what should Aunt Violet be doing in Blackpool, of all places?" Helen asked.

He stopped rummaging among the papers and let his hands fall to his sides in a curious gesture of failure and helplessness.

"I wish I knew, I wish I understood," he said. "It hasn't been at all as I'd . . . . But I mustn't start on that. It's so easy to become bitter when life deals one blow after blow. I'm sure Violet hasn't meant to hurt me in any way. It must be my own fault somehow. When the same thing happens to one over and over again in one's life, it must be because it's somehow in one's own nature, don't you think? . . . Look, here's the postcard."

He held out to Helen a gaudily coloured picture of the Blackpool illuminations.

"Read it," he said.

She turned it over. All that was written there, besides the address, was, "Weather very cold here but bracing. Will write soon, Violet." There was no address of a hotel or boarding-house.

Helen handed it back to him.

"What is it that happens to you over and over again?" she asked.

"Why, the way my marriages have turned out such disappointments." He saw something in Helen's face and went on, "Surely you knew I'd been married before? Violet must have mentioned it. I've been married twice before, as a matter of fact. Both of them wonderful women. I never really understood what they saw in me."

"Then——" Helen fumbled with the words. "They left you?"

Mignon broke in, "No, never. That's what's so wonderful. They've always sent him comforting messages and assurances of their love. It's my great privilege and a great happiness to me that those messages come through me."

He smiled wryly at Helen. "Yes, that's true, it *is* very wonderful. But perhaps we're rather puzzling you by our way of putting things. You see, Mignon and I very seldom speak of death."

"Then you mean—they died?" Helen tried to convince herself that a prickling feeling of cold had not spread down her spine.

"Yes," he said, "the other two did. At least, they *went away*. And Violet—she's gone away too. But she's been crueller than the others, because she could have stayed."

"And now," Mignon said eagerly, "you must tell me, I must know, it's of the greatest importance—what did

70

Violet say to you about the red-covered book and the
spectacles? Did Mr. Delborne keep them in the drawer
of his bedside table?"

"No," Helen said.

IX

LATER, IN the train back to London, Helen tried to think
out why she had lied to Mignon Colliver.

At the time of doing so, she had felt obscurely that she
was protecting her aunt. But now she realised that she
had also been protecting herself. She had been protecting
herself from entering on an argument and almost certainly
losing her temper, which had already been so frayed by
the annoyances of the week-end that she had suddenly
felt extraordinarily afraid of what might happen if she
lost control of herself.

For, as she saw it, the cheat that Mignon Colliver
had worked on her sister-in-law, and for all that Helen
knew, on her brother as well, was so blatant, so crude
and so heartless that she remained in a muttering state
of anger about it for the rest of the day.

It was obvious how Mignon had done it.

There were several women in the village who at
different times had worked as charwomen at Shipley's
End and any of whom might be able to tell her what Mr.
Delborne had kept in the drawer of his bedside table
and in less accessible drawers and cupboards. They would
be able to tell her innumerable things about his personal
habits, and most of them would have been more than
willing to supply this information, either in a flow of
innocent gossip, or, in one or two cases, for a small bribe.
Mignon then had used this knowledge of the dead man's
private life to convince her sister-in-law that she was in
communication with him.

That she would not have succeeded in this if Violet
Colliver, credulous, lonely, used to being bullied by a
stronger will than her own but not used to trickery,

71

had not wanted to be convinced, was probably true. If she had not found it consoling to believe that the man to whom she had given thirty years of her life was still troubling to send her messages and no doubt orders, she might have been more suspicious. But that did not lessen the cruelty of the trick, and Helen knew that it would have been impossible for her even to start discussing the red book and the spectacles with Mignon Colliver without speaking her mind.

But what would have been the good of doing that?

It was unlikely that she could have frightened such a cold-blooded and probably experienced trickster as Mignon into repentance or even into caution. It was unlikely also, supposing that Elvin was his sister's dupe, that he would have allowed himself to be convinced of this by Helen. And if he were not her dupe but her collaborator, the two of them would simply have produced a united front, faintly hurt, perhaps, but very tolerant towards Helen's unbelief and unkindness. Most important of all, an explosion of anger would not have helped her to discover why Aunt Violet had gone to Blackpool.

If she *had* gone to Blackpool . . .

At that point, left to herself, Helen would probably have abandoned her aunt to her fate. Aunt Violet, after all, had shown no signs of particularly welcoming her interference. She had sent her no postcard from Blackpool. With a busy week ahead of her, Helen might have put the whole disconcerting business out of her head until what was one day printed in all the newspapers shocked it back again.

But three days after her return from Burnstone, she had a visitor.

She had just returned from the art-school, taken off her hat and coat and lit the gas-fire when the bell rang. She was not expecting anyone and thought first that it was the tenant from the flat below, who took in her laundry for her and generally brought it upstairs when she heard Helen's footsteps overhead. Then she remembered that this was not the day for the laundry. Going to the door, she thought of Martin. She had an idea that she would see him again soon. He would be feeling a need at the moment, she thought, to explain to her what his mother had been doing in Burnstone in the company of Harold Hovard.

But the man whom she saw emerge from the shadows of the staircase was not Martin. It was Nicholas Dreydel.

He was in the same clothes as she had seen him in at Burnstone, and had the same look of having just come in from a country walk, except for the look of strain on his face.

When she exclaimed in surprise at seeing him, he said, " I telephoned two or three times during the afternoon, but there wasn't any answer, so I came out here and the woman in the flat below told me that you'd probably be in about now. Is it very inconvenient? I needn't take much of your time, though I'd like to ask you to have dinner with me."

His deep voice was flat and toneless, as if he were very tired.

Asking him in, Helen said that she would be glad to have dinner with him and offered him a drink and a cigarette while she went to change.

" Look, don't bother about that," he said. " I'm not dressed for it either. Let's go right away. I've a taxi waiting."

" All right." She picked up her coat. She nearly made a gibing remark about his impatience to start asking questions again, then for some reason she kept it to herself. He was not looking just then like a man who would be either amused or stung by it. " I was at Burnstone again last week-end," she said as they went down the stairs. " I didn't see you."

" I know. I was away all day," he said. " I went on a wild goose chase to Hampshire."

" To Burtonlea? "

" Yes. I heard you'd been there the day before."

" Yes, and I thought I was expected," Helen said. " I'd been there the week-end before and arranged with Aunt Violet to visit her again. She seemed lonely and anxious to see me and she was going to book a room and all. And then she just skipped out."

"But you did see her the week-end before? You actually saw her?"

"Yes, yes, yes!" Helen exclaimed. "Everybody asks that. I saw her, I talked to her. Why d'you doubt it?"

"I don't," he said. They got into the taxi and he gave an address in Soho. "I merely wanted a point to start from. Something certain. She *was* in Burtonlea ten days ago."

"I thought perhaps you'd been listening to disgraceful hints from Mrs. Andras," Helen said.

He smiled.

"I listened," he said. "It would have been difficult not to listen."

"So it was like that, was it?"

"Well, you wouldn't attempt to describe her as one of your best friends, would you?"

"No," Helen said with a sharp sigh. "No, I shouldn't."

"I shouldn't let it worry you," he said. "She isn't the type that gets taken seriously. For some reason she's mad to get that house and she lets everyone see that, which isn't the best way to recommend her unprejudiced point of view."

"Then you think she *is* mad to get the house?"

"No doubt about it."

The taxi shot into the narrow streets of Soho and stopped outside a small French restaurant. Helen and Dreydel went in and a waiter showed them to a table for two and brought the menu. While Dreydel was ordering, Helen thought about the change in him, the look of strain, of being near the end of his tether. He showed the signs too of being what she had not at all suspected at their earlier meeting, a desperately unhappy man.

As the waiter left them to fetch their cocktails, she said, "Now let's not put it off. Please tell me why you wanted to see me."

"I wanted to see you because I've been thinking about you a great deal," he answered sombrely. "I've been thinking about telling you a story and seeing what

you make of it. You might be able to tell me if
I'm half off my head or if my brain's still got some
grip on reality."

" That sounds like a big responsibility you want me to
take."

" Do you mind ? "

" It's about those two women, isn't it ? "

" Yes," he said. " I could have told you the whole
story last time, only I didn't know how you'd take a
thing like that from a complete stranger. Now——"
He gave the quick smile that for a very short moment took
the hardness and gravity out of his face. " We're still
strangers, of course, if you want to labour the point."

" Well, go on," she said.

He nodded, but hesitated as if he still had to search
for words. The waiter brought them their drinks then,
so it was a minute or two before the story started. During
the interruption, Helen saw how one of Dreydel's hands,
lying on the table, tightened into a fist. But when he
started to talk, it gradually relaxed.

" I may as well start at the end," he said, " and tell
you that I suspect Elvin Colliver of having murdered two
wives and of preparing now, if he hasn't done it already,
to murder his third wife. His motive, of course, has always
been their money. His second wife is the one with whom
I'm most concerned. Her name was Lillian Lander.
She was a widow with a moderate income and a daughter,
Evelyn. I was in love with Evelyn. We were engaged to
be married."

He looked at Helen questioningly, as if he were uncertain that she could have taken in what he had said.

" But she had some other name when you told me about
her before," she said. " Lillian, I mean."

" Yes, Poplar," he said. " He was calling himself
George Poplar. Evelyn was very unhappy about the
marriage. I'd gone back to Africa again and Evelyn
was to have followed me in about a year's time. Poplar
hadn't even been on the scene while I was in England.
Then only a few weeks after I left, Evelyn wrote that her
mother had gone on a holiday to Worthing, met this man

and married him by special licence almost immediately. He was a widower whose first wife had been killed in a motor-accident. Or that was his story. Evelyn was suspicious of him from the start. She said that he was one of the most unconvincing charlatans she'd ever met. So she did her best to check up on the story, but the trouble was that so far as she could make out, the accident that he had described had never happened, or anyway, not to any woman called Poplar. But her mother was infatuated and deliriously happy, and of course, in the traditional way, let him handle all her money. Then she died."

" In an accident ? "

" Yes. At the inquest the doubt of its being anything but an accident was hardly raised. Evelyn tried to get the police to listen to her suspicions, but while they were arguing about it, Poplar disappeared. He disappeared with nearly all his wife's money. She hadn't changed her will and what she had left came to Evelyn, but in fact he'd got hold of nearly all of it before he killed her. I came home then. I got some special leave and flew home. I tried to get Evelyn to marry me immediately and go back with me. But she had a crazy idea she had to find her mother's murderer. She wouldn't listen."

" And you couldn't stay on ? "

" No. That is . . ." The deep voice grated for a moment. " Who knows what one might have done— what one would have done—if one could have seen a little way into the future ? The fact is, we quarrelled. I suppose each of us was hurt that the other wouldn't do what we wanted. From then on, Evelyn's letters changed. For one thing, there weren't so many of them and as time went on they got fewer and fewer. And they said less and less. And then they stopped."

" And you accepted it ? "

" What else could I have done ? The last letter I ever had from her reached me a little over a year ago. Of course at the time, I didn't know it was going to be the last letter. It was pretty impersonal. By then I think we'd both got round to assuming that marriage was off.

I answered the letter as usual, but when I didn't hear any more from her, well . . ."

Helen nodded.

"The next thing that happened," he went on, "was a letter, about six months later, from a friend of Evelyn's. The friend was an American woman and the letter came from San Francisco. I'd never met her, but Evelyn had often spoken about her. I knew she'd got married some time before and that she and her husband had had their honeymoon in Europe. As a matter of fact, in Evelyn's last letter, she mentioned that they'd be arriving in England in a few days' time and how much she was looking forward to seeing them. Well, this friend—her name's Odette Gooderman—wrote and asked me if I knew what had happened to Evelyn, because she'd not only stopped answering her letters but now they were coming back to her, marked 'Gone Away.' So I wrote to Evelyn and my letter came back too. I tried cabling and that was no good either. I wrote to one or two friends of hers and they seemed to be surprised to hear that she wasn't out in Gambia with me. Meanwhile, I'd been corresponding with Mrs. Gooderman and she'd told me a very curious story."

He leant back in his chair, giving Helen another long, questioning look. "Clear, so far?"

"Perfectly," she said.

"You're a patient listener. Well, what Mrs. Gooderman told me was this. When she and her husband were in England, they'd gone on a number of long, sightseeing drives and once they'd taken Evelyn with them. They'd gone to Oxford and then on into the Cotswolds and they were driving through a village called Burnstone when Evelyn caught sight of a man in the garden of an old house—a very beautiful old house, Mrs. Gooderman said, and its name was Shipley's End. Evelyn had suddenly got wildly excited, saying, ' There he is—that's the man ! ' And she'd insisted on getting out of the car immediately. But she'd insisted also on their going on, because she said her business with this man wouldn't be over quickly, and so after a bit of argument, they'd driven on. And that

77

was the last they'd seen of her. She was standing at the gate of Shipley's End, talking to this man."

" Elvin Colliver ? "

" What do you think ? The police say no, it wasn't."

" Then you've been to the police ? "

" Oh yes, as soon as I got home. As soon as I'd been to her old lodgings and discovered that she'd never come home from Burnstone. The landlady wasn't a good type and when Evelyn disappeared, owing about a month's rent, it never occurred to the woman to go to the police. She'd just quietly helped herself to Evelyn's belongings—to make up for the money that was owed her, as she put it. But I stirred the police up and they've hunted for Evelyn high and low and they can't find a trace of her. Nobody in Burnstone appears to have seen her, or if they ever did, they aren't letting on. And the police say it's impossible that Elvin Colliver could have been George Poplar."

" Why do they say that ? "

" Because they're been into Colliver's history and they say that at the time when Poplar was living with Evelyn's mother, Colliver was living with his sister and an invalid wife in Southsea. They admit that Colliver was often away from home, but they claim that that was because he was part of some phony table-rapping sort of act. In fact, he got into trouble for it and though he and his sister still dabble in it, they're very careful now about how far they go."

" And George Poplar—was he often away from home too ? "

He gave a grim laugh.

" You take a point quickly," he said. " George Poplar was some sort of commercial traveller."

Helen pressed her hands together under the table. They felt cold and damp.

" You never saw him, did you ? " she said. " Poplar, I mean."

" No."

" Nor a photograph of him ? "

" No. I've only got Evelyn's description of him. He

was a smallish, rather plump man, with a pasty complexion and dark hair, It fits, doesn't it ? "

" Yes. What about fingerprints ? "

He looked puzzled at the question.

She explained, " When Poplar disappeared straight after his wife's death, with all her money, didn't the police do anything at all ? Didn't they think there was anything suspicious about it ? "

" Oh yes," he said. " In fact, I think they came round to agreeing with Evelyn that her mother had been murdered, though they couldn't prove a thing about the accident. And as for fingerprints—there weren't any. Poplar had done a very thorough job, suggesting, among other things, practice. You see, he'd suffered from some sort of eczema on his hands, or claimed that he did, and he'd always worn gloves, grey, cotton gloves."

Those words, more than any others he had yet used, gave Helen the sense of cold, deliberate evil, working with what amounted to devotion towards its horrible and carefully premeditated end.

" All the same, there's something that doesn't fit— there's something all wrong somewhere ! " she exclaimed. " That man Poplar you've been describing, a man who'd keep a pair of gloves on for months because he knew that at the end of them he was going to commit a murder, a man as careful as that, would never marry Aunt Violet."

" I should have thought she was just the sort that he would marry," Dreydel said. " From all I've heard of her, she's very like Evelyn's mother, a good, unsuspicious, not very clever, lonely woman."

" Yes, but don't you see, Aunt Violet hasn't any money. The house and the money aren't hers. When she dies, they go to Mrs. Andras. Alive, Aunt Violet may be useful, in a modest way, to a designing husband, but dead her value's quite gone. He'd gain nothing whatever by murdering her."

" I can only suggest then," Dreydel said, " that your aunt, in her anxiety to acquire a husband, may have quietly suppressed the true facts about her property. Or she may even be so unworldly that she's never really understood them herself and so misled him unintentionally."

" Oh no, not Aunt Violet. She understood that much and she'd never have kept it to herself."

" But don't you think she's been behaving, for this past year, as if she were suspicious of Colliver. Not quite certain about him, perhaps, but all the same, suspicious and afraid. And you might consider the relationship between certain dates. A year ago Evelyn got out of her friends' car and went to speak to a man in the garden of Shipley's End and was never seen again. A year ago your aunt went quietly away, as if life there had suddenly become intolerable. A year ago the garden of Shipley's End was first allowed to get out of hand—I know that, because when Odette Gooderman saw it it was still beautiful. She described it in one of her letters as being a typical English garden, all beautifully kept lawns and roses, even in October. But after that time, the weeds took over. Nobody touched them."

" Then you think—you believe——" But Helen could not get the rest of the words out. Her voice dried up in her throat.

Dreydel finished the sentence for her. " I believe that that once lovely, typical English garden contains the bones of Evelyn Lander. And I believe that it's become a matter of desperate urgency for us to find your aunt. Because, don't you see, *that man's started gardening again.* He couldn't bury a body amongst all that weed without the signs of the digging betraying him, but when it's all been freshly dug——"

" Don't, don't ! " Helen exclaimed, her fists striking the table. " I understand you."

X

THE WAITER came and went. Helen, gripping the edge of the table, saw her finger-tips whiten from the pressure she was putting on them.

" She was scared," she said. " I know she was scared. Yet I'm sure it wasn't of her husband."

" What else might she have been afraid of ? " Dreydel asked.

" I don't know. But she spoke of her husband with love and admiration. He went to visit her often and she seemed to look forward to his visits, not to be afraid of them."

" What makes you so certain she was scared ? " he asked.

" Just a look in her eyes, a sound in her voice. I could have been mistaken. All the same . . ." She hesitated, then started to describe her visit to the guest-house.

After that, hardly noticing the transition, she went on to tell him a great deal about her aunt, about the old days in Burnstone when Mr. Delborne had been alive and about the time that she had spent there herself, when she and Martin had been children.

Partly she talked to keep away from the grim subject that Nicholas Dreydel had raised. Partly, she knew, she had another object. What this object was she did not precisely know, but as she talked about the garden as it had been in those days, she felt all the time that she was working her way round to something. Talking of how the spring came there, with a froth of white blossom on the thicket of wild plum and with crocuses and snowdrops in every crevice, she told him how, for a town-bred child, the cold days of March, with their sudden gleams of sunshine, had been charged with a never-to-be-forgotten excitement.

" The spring and the autumn," she said, " I never understood them, I never felt them until I lived down at Burnstone. It's true there's something lovely about spring in London, but still one never notices how early it begins, or in the same way, how long into the winter the autumn lingers. One tends to judge the seasons by the clothes one wears . . ." She stopped herself. "I don't know why I'm talking like this."

With his grave look, he answered, "I think it's to exorcise the horrors from a place you've loved very much. I'm sorry I brought those horrors with me."

"You didn't, it was Martin who brought them," she said. "It was he who suggested that Aunt Violet might be buried somewhere under all those weeds. I knew that couldn't be true, because I'd had a card from her only a few weeks before and those weeds had taken more than a few weeks to grow. But the idea must have stuck in my mind somehow, because now that you've made a suggestion so like it—except that I suppose yours could be true—I feel as if it's what I've been expecting."

But she had still not said what was at the back of her mind. The thought there that she wanted to grasp, to bring into the open, still eluded her, and presently she began to think that there had been nothing there as all. But contradictorily, thinking this, she became convinced that it had been something important.

Dreydel said, "Then you think my story could be true."

"I don't know. Not really. Perhaps." She felt hopelessly confused. "Before you told it to me, I'd more or less made up my mind that the dangerous person was Mignon Colliver and that her brother was simply her dupe. That seemed to me to make the best sense of the situation. You see, she keeps him supplied with spirit messages from his two dead wives, which makes her, naturally, a very important person in his life. And I thought she might have used some similar device for getting rid of Aunt Violet, or else, perhaps that Aunt Violet couldn't stand living in a sort of ghostly harem and so had cleared out. But that can't be right if your story's true. And if it's true, I still don't understand how the sort of man that Elvin Colliver must be could have made the blunder of marrying Aunt Violet, whose money he could never inherit, or, having made the blunder, what he had to gain by chasing her away. I suppose you've been to the police with your suggestion about the garden ? "

" Yes. But unfortunately the police are a little tired of me. As I said, they won't listen to the possibility that Colliver could be Poplar."

" I was wondering," she said, " do you know anything about the other two Mrs. Collivers ? You said something about his having had an invalid wife. Do you know how she died—and the other one too ? "

" The second one, the invalid, committed suicide," he said.

" Suicide ! "

" She took an overdose of some sleeping-tablets. It's only fair to mention, however, that she was dying of cancer and in great pain. The suicide could have been genuine."

" Did he inherit anything from her ? "

" Yes, two or three thousand pounds. Not a great deal. But murders have been done for far less. I don't know anything about the first wife."

" And you—you're absolutely convinced that he's Poplar and that he murdered Evelyn and Evelyn's mother ? "

" Yes."

" Suppose you're wrong ? "

" Then I shall have to begin all over again."

" But your leave won't last for ever."

" There are worse things than losing one's job. One is to carry the load on one's conscience that I've got on mine."

She crumbled some bread beside her plate. " I think you blame yourself too much."

He looked quickly into her eyes. " But it isn't really a question of blame, you know. It's just the feeling that one's failed someone—failed them to the limit. And that there's going to be no going back on it, no chance at all to put it right, but knowing that if one had had something that one didn't have—strength, understanding, God knows what—everything would have worked out differently. Probably nothing of that sort ever happened to you."

"I don't know." She looked away down the room. She found herself thinking uneasily of Martin. "Perhaps it did."

"Look at this." Dreydel took his wallet out of his pocket and out of it took a photograph which he handed across the table to Helen.

She felt a kind of embarrassment in looking at it. The photograph was a snapshot of himself and a girl standing side by side on a sunlit beach, with a view of rocks and glistening waves behind them. Both were laughing. Both looked utterly carefree and at ease. Dreydel looked many years younger than he did now. Helen could not help thinking about this more than about the unknown girl at his side, though she knew that she must say something about her.

"She's very beautiful," she said. This was true. Remembering his description of the girl's colouring, the red-brown hair, the golden-brown eyes, Helen thought that she must have been very beautiful indeed.

"Yes," he said. He waited for more.

"She's very tall," Helen said. "Almost as tall as you."

"Yes."

"Perhaps—perhaps you'll find her again."

He reached out and took the photograph back.

"What are you going to do next?" she asked.

"Find your aunt," he said. "Find her fast."

"But how are you going to set about that? You can't possibly go to every hotel in Blackpool."

"I don't think that will be necessary. From something you've told me, I think I know how to find her."

"From something *I* said?"

"Don't ask me about it yet. When I find her, I'll tell you."

That was all that he would say on the matter. He went on talking, but now suddenly of everyday things, as if it had just occurred to him to try to turn the evening into one like any other spent in a quiet Soho restaurant with a woman in whom he took a rather guarded interest.

Helen's effort to respond to this was even less convincing than his. She was trying to remember what she had said that could possibly help him to find her aunt and presently came to the conclusion that she had not in fact said anything that could be in the least useful in his search. For some reason then, she thought, he had wanted to mislead her.

But in that case, how much else of what he had told her had been misleading?

They left early. He insisted on seeing her home, although she protested that he should be thinking of a train back to Oxford.

" Or aren't you going back to-night ? " she asked.

" Oh yes, but there's a midnight train," he said.

" I thought perhaps you might be going to Blackpool."

" I doubt very much if I shall have to go to Blackpool at all," he said. " And going there now would be quite useless. But don't worry, I'll find Mrs. Colliver for you. I don't know where she is yet, but I know I can find her."

That was what he repeated, standing on the pavement outside the house where she lived, shaking her hand.

" Don't worry, I'll find Mrs. Colliver for you."

From behind Helen a sardonic voice said, " I'd like to wish you luck in that. May I know if you're serious ? "

Helen turned sharply. But she had recognised the voice and did not need to wait for the figure in the dark doorway to move forward into the light of the street-lamp to know that it was Martin Andras.

Stiffly she introduced the two men. She saw a quick interest appear on Dreydel's face when he heard Martin's name, but on Martin's face there was something both suspicious and mocking, and knowing the meaning of that look, Helen hoped that Dreydel would get back into his taxi and go before Martin began to demonstrate just how rude and offensive he could be when the humour took him.

Perhaps she showed this clearly, for Dreydel's face changed as he glanced from Martin back to her. She could not read his new expression and when he had gone, as he had immediately, and she was fumbling in her bag for her key, the thought of the strangeness in his face during those last few moments troubled her. As if her uncertainty in groping after the meaning of it had got into her fingers, they groped helplessly about in her bag until Martin took it from her.

"Here, let me," he said, and found the key at once. "Now do I come in or do I stay outside?"

"Whichever you like," she said.

"I've been waiting hours," he said. "What have you been doing, hiring yourself a detective?"

"Why did you wait?" she asked. "I wasn't expecting you."

"I wanted to see you. Who is that man, Helen? Is he a detective?"

"Of course not."

"Then why's he going to find your aunt for you?"

"He seems to want to."

"For God's sake!"

"Well, he's got his own reasons, which I'll tell you if you want to listen to them." She thrust her key into the lock. "Are you coming in?"

"I didn't like the look of him," Martin said. "If he's a detective, I shouldn't trust him too far."

"He isn't a detective."

She went upstairs, Martin following her.

He went on questioning her about Dreydel. Downstairs she had felt ready to tell him all that he wanted to know, but his mere insistence stopped her. Starting to answer evasively, shrugging her shoulders, she acted as if there really were some secret about Dreydel.

That was how she might have continued and Martin, tense, restless and with every moment more antagonistic, might have worked himself up into making some unbearable scene, or else might abruptly have left her without ever telling her why he had come, if she had not caught sight of his face at a particular moment.

Startled, she exclaimed, "Why, Martin, what's the matter?"

His dark, bright eyes were desperate, far too desperate,

she realised now, for the mere sight of her with Dreydel to have been the cause of it.

" You don't want to know," he answered. " You don't give a damn."

She went closer to him. As she looked curiously into his face she noticed how pale it was.

" What is it ? " she repeated.

He jerked away from her. Walking half-way across the room to the door, he turned and came back.

" All right, I came here because I thought I could talk to you, I thought you could help," he said. " I thought if I could talk to anyone it'd be you, but you don't want me to.

She did not answer at once. She wondered how she could have failed for a moment to see that he was in trouble and that his strange and unreasonable show of jealousy or whatever it had been, had been his way of demanding help.

" Is that why you came the other night—because you needed help ? " she asked.

" Suppose it was ? " he said.

" Why didn't you say so ? "

" Is it ever an easy thing to say ? And you were looking at me as if you could hardly wait for me to leave."

" No," she said. " No, I didn't understand."

" There wasn't much to understand. It was only a question of whether or not you wanted to see me. But I knew which it was as soon as I saw you."

She put a hand to her forehead. " *I* didn't," she said. " I didn't know which it was and I don't know now. I only know I want to keep everything very clear and simple between us. I couldn't bear anything else now."

" When was anything ever clear and simple ? " Martin asked. " I've never found anything that was. That may be my fault. It may be what I make of things. But if it is, there isn't much chance that I'll ever alter, is there ? So it isn't much use my trying to talk."

" But why don't you ? Why don't you tell me about this trouble you're in ? "

" *I'm* not in any trouble." He said it sharply, in a

tone of surprise. But as he went on there was a sound of confusion in his voice. " Perhaps I am, though. Only I haven't been thinking about it as my trouble."

" Whose is it then—your mother's ? "

It was the wrong thing to have said. His face went blank.

" What made you ask that ? " he said.

" Then it isn't hers ? "

" Any troubles she has, she keeps to herself," he said with a curious grimness.

" Well, if you don't want to tell me . . ."

" Helen, please ! " There was a wild appeal in the two words. Then his arms went round her and he pulled her to him.

At first she was startled and stiff, but then her body relaxed against his and a tide of warmth flowed through her. After the first instant he held her gently, not kissing her but pressing his face down into her hair.

Then he said softly into her ear something that at that moment sounded to her wholly incredible, " Helen, we've *got* to find your aunt ! "

She jerked away from him.

" *Damn my aunt !* " she cried.

" Yes," he said perfectly seriously and she saw that his face was as haggard as ever. " Yes, but we've got to find her. You think I—we don't want to find her because of that miserable house and money. I tell you, I wish to God there wasn't any house and money ! We don't need it, we don't want it."

She felt as if her own breathing were choking her.

" Then is that what you came here to say ? "

" No—yes. Oh, what does it matter ? That man— that man who said he was going to find her—is he going to ? Why don't you want to tell me about him ? "

She walked away from him to a chair. She sat down, leaning back. After a moment she started to tell him all about Dreydel. She thought that he listened only for the first minute or two, but she went on and while she talked her composure came back. But now it was true that she could hardly wait for him to leave.

When she stopped he surprised her by smiling suddenly. "Bluebeard Colliver," he said. She realised that he had played his old trick of seeming to pay no attention and yet taking in most of what had been said. "Do you believe it?"

"It's what you suggested yourself," she said.

"So I did," he said. "But you didn't believe me."

"No. And now—now I think that you didn't even believe it yourself. You didn't, did you, Martin?"

"In any case, I was wrong."

"But all along you knew you were wrong." She spoke with certainty now, her excitement rising. "All along you only wanted to stir me up to find her for you. I don't know why it was so important to you, or why it's so important to you to find her now, but that was why you came here first and now again to-night. . . . And this trouble you're in, I believe it's only that for some mysterious reason you've got to find Aunt Violet."

"If your friend Dreydel's right," he said, "it's a rather important thing to do, isn't it?"

"But that isn't why you want to find her."

"Sometimes you're so wrong about me, Helen," he answered. "Sometimes you're so awfully wrong. Well, we'll see which of us will find her first, Dreydel or me."

He started towards the door.

"Martin——" she began.

It did not stop him.

As Helen heard him running down the stairs she thought for a moment that she was going to start crying, but without knowing whether it would be tears of anger, of wretchedness or simple exhaustion. The feeling passed and jumping up she found herself a cigarette, lit it and drew at it fiercely.

"Dreydel will find her," she said aloud and all of a sudden was certain that he would.

XI

It took Nicholas Dreydel nearly three weeks to find Mrs. Colliver.

During that time Helen heard nothing from him. She did not even know for sure that he was really trying to find her aunt. She saw no more of Martin but she had a short letter from him.

It said, " Sorry about the other evening. I've got a lot on my mind, but when I try to talk about it, I mess it up. Try to forgive me."

Also she had another postcard from Mrs. Colliver. It showed the same view of Blackpool as the one that she had sent to her husband and, like his, gave no address. It said merely that she was well and would write again soon. Helen propped the postcard against a vase on the mantelpiece and from time to time picked it up and re-read it. It always revived the same disquiet.

The withholding of an address a fortnight after Mrs. Colliver had arrived in Blackpool could only have been deliberate. Yet how could Helen have become involved in whatever had terrified her aunt and sent her into hiding ? For that was what Helen now believed must have happened. Something that she had said or done that day in Hampshire must have worked on her aunt's fears in such a manner as to make her feel that she could not face seeing Helen again. But searching her memory told Helen nothing.

Then Dreydel telephoned. It was late one evening and Helen was already in bed, reading for a little before settling down to sleep. When the bell started ringing she was immediately certain who was making the call and expected to hear the operator's voice telling her that the call was from Blackpool. Instead it was Dreydel's voice that spoke at once.

" I'm sorry to disturb you so late," he said, " but I've

traced your aunt and I wanted to tell you what's happened."

"Where are you?" she asked.

"In Barnet."

"D'you mean to say that that's where my aunt is—here in London?" Helen said.

"Yes, her address is 11 Highfield Gardens, Barnet. It's a small semi-detached house and she seems to be living in it alone."

"Is she all right?"

"I don't know. I caught a glimpse of her when she came to the door, but I haven't spoken to her yet. I wanted to ask you if you could come out here to-morrow. I'd be very grateful if you'd go with me to see her."

"I'm working to-morrow," Helen said. "I shan't be free till about five."

"Suppose I meet you soon after five then. Where shall I wait for you?"

"What about Leicester Square station? . . . But just a minute. How did you find her?"

"By keeping an eye on Colliver and waiting till he came to see her. You told me that he often went to see her in Hampshire and I thought that sooner or later he'd do it again. Actually I think he came here last week but he managed to give me the slip. I must have blundered somehow because I don't think he knew I was watching him."

"Then he's with her now?" Helen could make no sense of it. She had thought that this time her aunt had run away from her husband as well as from her niece.

"No," Dreydel said. "He came up on an afternoon train and spent the evening with her. He left about ten minutes ago, I think to catch that midnight train back to Oxford."

"And she's all right?" Helen was suddenly intensely anxious at the thought that Elvin Colliver had spent a whole evening in a house alone with his wife. "You're sure she's all right still?"

"She came to the door when he left," Dreydel said.

" I caught a glimpse of her standing there and he kissed her good-bye."

" And she's been in London all the time," Helen said wonderingly. " Whatever has she been doing in London ? "

" I can make a guess," Dreydel said. " At any rate, I know this, that if I wanted a place to disappear in, I'd choose a London suburb where I didn't know anyone. Good night now. I'll see you to-morrow."

" Good night," she said and slowly put the telephone down.

Next day, at a quarter past five, she met Dreydel at the booking-office of the Leicester Square Underground station. He was waiting for her when she arrived. He took two tickets to Barnet and they went down the escalator together. The rush-hour had already begun and stairs and platform were so crowded that it was almost impossible to say more than a few sentences to one another, and in the train they had to stand. As they stood wedged close together in the crowd in the swaying train, Dreydel said in her ear, " I'll tell you the rest of it when we get to the other end."

" Then there's some more than you told me last night ? " she asked.

" A little. Suppose we have a quick drink before we go on to the house."

Someone struggling towards the doors as the train drew up at a station thrust his way between them and they gave up the attempt to talk.

At Barnet, as soon as they got out of the train, a sharp wind cut at them. It seemed to Helen that the evening had suddenly become far colder than it had been in the centre of London. It was as if, during the short time spent in the train, they had made the journey from autumn to winter. Faces seen in the lamplight had a pinched, chilled look. Finding herself shivering, she was very glad to turn in at the door of the first pub they came to.

Yet inside, sitting close to a fire, the shivering did not quite cease. So it was nerves, she told herself. She was in the grip of some excitement or dread, which made it difficult to sit still. After all, it would have been easier to have gone straight on, struggling against the wind, to 11 Highfield Gardens.

"What I wanted to tell you," Dreydel said, as he brought their drinks from the bar to the fireside, " is that I think someone else had the same idea as I did. I think someone else has been watching Colliver."

" Someone else ? "

" Your young friend Andras."

As he said it, she saw on his face the same curious expression that she had seen there at the time of his meeting with Martin. Perhaps it was no more than an intense watchfulness, but it heightened her uneasiness, and gave her a feeling that it was of the greatest importance to show no particular surprise, to reply casually.

" He's been very anxious about my aunt," she said. " I know he's been trying to find her too."

" I've been told," Dreydel said, " that you and he are engaged to be married."

It was not what she had been expecting and she thought that her cheeks coloured.

" No," she said. " At one time we thought about it. But that's long ago."

" I see. And he's very attached to your aunt, is he ? "

" Oh, quite, I think." She still had the feeling that she must be casual about it, but by now she knew why she felt this. She did not want this man, about whom, after all, she knew nothing at all, except what he had chosen to tell her, asking her questions about Martin's motives, perhaps tricking her somehow into revealing that she herself did not understand them. It was an urge to protect her old friend, her old love, from the stranger.

All at once she wished that she had not agreed to go with this man whom she did not know to see her aunt. She wished that she had stayed away from work that day and without having told him what she intended to do, come out here by herself in the morning. But it was too late for that now.

As if he knew what was in her mind, Dreydel stopped

his questioning. She thought that he looked put out. Finishing his drink quickly, he said, " Shall we go now ? "

" You haven't told me yet why you want to see my aunt," she said. " Are you going to try to persuade her that her husband's a mass murderer ? "

" Something like that," he said.

" I don't think you'll find it easy."

" I'm counting on you to help me."

" But you do understand," she said as they went to the door, " that I'm far from convinced of it myself ? "

" You can tell her so," he said. " Nobody's going to stop you."

They went out together into the cold and the driving wind.

Highfield Gardens was a long street of small, semi-detached houses, of the type built in the years before the second world war. Some were of plain brick and some were covered with roughcast, but all had bay windows with plenty of stained glass in them and small, neat front gardens with asphalt pathways to neat front doors. Along the edge of each pavement small trees had been planted. Their slim trunks curved before the force of the wind. Where there were lights in rooms the curtains of which had not been drawn, each house presented an almost identical scene, a dining-room furnished with a shiny dark oak dining-room suite, with an embroidered runner on the table and a bevelled mirror hanging above a fireplace of fantastically coloured tiles.

The house they wanted was at the far end of the street. It had the words " Number Eleven," done on a fretwork panel, over the front door. The whole of the front garden had been cunningly laid out as a rockery, decorated with a couple of gnomes and a stone rabbit. It was the kind of house, Helen thought, for which it was possible that her aunt had always had a secret longing, finding it far closer to her requirements and her true taste than a great old house with thick stone walls, cold stone floors and beamed ceilings that eternally trailed cobwebs.

But at the moment there was something disturbing

about it. Behind the curtained windows there was no sign of a light.

"It looks as if she's out," Helen said, stopping at the gate.

"Better ring and make sure, though," Dreydel said.

They went up the asphalt path and Helen put a finger on the brightly polished brass bell-push. They heard the bell ring shrilly in the house. But no one came to answer it.

"Try again," Dreydel said.

Helen rang three times, but there was still no answer.

"She may have gone to the pictures," she said. "She likes doing that. She goes at five and comes home for a latish supper."

"In that case perhaps we should go and have dinner ourselves and come back afterwards," he said.

Helen agreed. Yet they both lingered, as if by doing so they could somehow still make contact with Mrs. Colliver. While they stood there, they heard the sound of a door banging in the wind.

They looked at each other questioningly, each wanting to know if the other had heard it. The door banged again.

"She's left something open," Helen said. "The back door or a garden door."

"Let's go and see," Dreydel said and set off round the house, along a path that ran between the house and a small wooden coal-shed, then disappeared ahead of them into the darkness of the garden at the back of the house.

The door that was banging was at the side of the house, a door that led straight into a small kitchen. As they reached it, it shut sharply in their faces, then more slowly swung open again.

Dreydel put a hand on it, holding it.

"Do we go in?" he said.

Helen was frowning, thinking that there was something very strange about the fact that Aunt Violet, after a lifetime of locking doors, shooting bolts and carefully fastening chains, because Mr. Delborne had always suspected that the respectable workpeople of Hovard and

Hayle would one night try to burgle his house, should have gone out and left the back door unlocked.

" I think perhaps we'd better," she said. " She may have been taken ill."

Dreydel pushed the door open and stepped inside. Helen followed him.

When he had found the light-switch and turned it on, he closed the door. The kitchen was a small one, with black and white checked linoleum on the floor, a porcelain sink with shiny chromium taps, a pre-war gas-cooker and a built-in dresser. Everything was tidy, the sink clean, the sink-basket empty. Two tea-cloths were hanging on the clothes-airer, the dish-cloth had been wrung out and was hanging over the edge of the sink. The only object at all out of place was a full milk-bottle, which was on the draining-board, as if it had been fetched in from the doorstep and set down there and forgotten, instead of put away in the larder.

From the kitchen Dreydel and Helen went quickly into the small hall, turning on the light, which shone murkily inside a lantern of amber-coloured glass on to more linoleum and a branching hat-stand. There were two doorways and a straight, steep staircase.

Dreydel and Helen looked first into the front room. It was a dining-room like all the other dining-rooms they had seen, a table in the centre with an embroidered runner on it, four chairs round it, a sideboard with a bowl of fruit on it, and a tiled fireplace of an extraordinary shape with a single-bar electric fire in front of its empty hearth. It had the faintly musty smell of a room that is seldom used, but was so clean that it had certainly been swept and dusted that morning.

The back room was more interesting.

First, it was slightly warmed by the remains of a fire. In the darkness before Dreydel had turned on the light, the cinders had glowed redly, though in the light there was little to be seen in the grate but the tumbled ash. The room was a sitting-room, furnished with the inevitable two arm-chairs and sofa, covered in imitation leather with velvet cushions. Over the fireplace there was a print of ducks flying into a sunset. The curtains, of some kind of artificial silk, were a gingery brown. But there were positive signs in the room that it had been inhabited by Mrs. Colliver.

There was her old work-basket on a table, with a piece of embroidery and her spectacles lying beside it. There was her knitting-bag hanging on the arm of a chair. There was her leather writing-case, with her initials stamped on it, which had been a present to her from Martin and Helen, that Christmas of nineteen forty, when they were first at Burnstone together. There was one of her slippers, lying in the middle of the hearth-rug. There was her handbag, an untidy, bulging affair, also on the floor, propped against the corner of the arm-chair by the fire, the velvet cushion of which still showed the impress of her weight. There was a tray on a low, bandy-legged coffee-table near the chair. On the tray were a bottle of sherry, a bottle of gin, a bottle of lime-juice and two glasses. Both glasses had been used. In one were the dregs of some sherry. The other was half full of a colourless liquid, presumably gin.

Very puzzled, Helen said, " But she wouldn't go out without her handbag."

" Let's look upstairs," Dreydel said, and went out quickly, taking the stairs two at a time.

They looked into each of the three cold, neat bedrooms, the bathroom and even into the linen-cupboard. But there was no question about it, Mrs. Colliver was not in the house. Nor was her second slipper.

Several other pairs of shoes, all on trees and carefully polished, were in a row on the floor of her wardrobe and her old fur coat was inside it too, on a hanger. Her hat, her one and only unchanging hat, was on the top shelf of the wardrobe.

Helen pointed out these things to Dreydel.

" So it looks," he said, " as if your Aunt Violet, without her hat, her coat or her handbag, fled from this house by the back-door with only one shoe on and without waiting to shut the door behind her. Or else . . ." He stopped.

Helen turned sharply from the wardrobe to look at him. His face had gone colourless, his mouth was grim and his eyes were furious.

Yet it was with a curious gentleness that he spoke next, laying a hand on her arm and drawing her towards the door.

" Come, let's go down and think this out."

She went with him without saying anything. She had a sick feeling, and a throbbing in her temples. They went back to the sitting-room. Dreydel stood looking down at the tray of drinks with a heavy though absent-minded frown on his face. With one fist he pounded the palm of his other hand.

Helen had a confused feeling that the tray, with its two used glasses, ought to tell her something, but her thoughts had gone chasing off after something else.

" Look," she said, " I've an idea what could have happened. Suppose someone—one of the neighbours—came to the back door, suddenly needing help of some sort. I mean a real emergency, an accident in their house, or something. Well, if that happened, Aunt Violet might easily run out of the house, just as she was, for-getting to shut the back door. And stay with them until she wasn't needed any longer."

She was speaking jerkily, hastily. Dreydel seemed to make an effort to pay attention to her.

" And the second slipper ? " he said.

" She may have kept some spare shoes or rubber boots or something in the kitchen—for going to the dust-bin and fetching coal and so on. Perhaps she stopped long enough just to kick off her slippers and put on the others. And the other slipper may have fallen outside the door. We might find it out there on the path if we looked."

" In that case," Dreydel said, " this slipper "—he pointed at the one on the hearthrug—" would be in the kitchen."

" Unless she lost it in her hurry to get to the door when she heard the knocking. Or perhaps she wasn't wearing the slippers at all and just picked one up as she went and dropped it somewhere."

She could see that she was making no impression on him at all.

But he said, "All right, let's go and look outside."

They went out to the kitchen again, opening the back door and stepped out into the darkness.

At that moment the wind had dropped and the evening had become very quiet. The sounds that reached them seemed to come from a long way off, the noise of traffic on the main road, the slurred sound of the trolley-buses, the rattle of a tube train, someone whistling in the distance. But close at hand there was silence.

In that silence they heard quite plainly the faint little cry that came from the coal-shed.

Dreydel's hand shot out to the door. But it was locked. Cursing, he tore at it, making the whole flimsy structure shake, while an eerie wail went up inside it.

Helen darted back into the kitchen. She had remembered something that she had seen there, a key hanging on a hook just inside the door. She snatched the key and ran back to Dreydel. He took the key from her with hands that were shaking, fitted it into the lock and pulled the door open.

Quite unreasonably, Helen wanted to scream when a small black kitten shot out of the coalshed, sliding against her ankles and disappearing into the house.

XII

THEY MADE a perfunctory search for the slipper but found nothing. Any dim faith that Helen had had in her own theory had faded at sight of the kitten. It had not been her aunt who had left the poor little creature locked in the coalshed. Nor could it have been that imaginary neighbour who needed help in a desperate hurry.

Going back into the house, Helen and Dreydel found the kitten in the kitchen. Its paws, black with coal-dust, had made a criss-cross pattern on the clean linoleum. It had gone into hiding behind a bucket and took a moment to make up its mind to trust the intruders, but then it came sidling out to rub its sooty fur against Helen's stockings, crying pitifully.

" It's hungry," she said and reached out a hand towards the milk-bottle on the draining-board.

" Wait," Dreydel said. " Just possibly we ought not to touch that bottle."

" Aunt Violet wouldn't mind . . ." Then she realised what he had meant. " But we've got to give the wretched little creature something to drink. God knows how long it's been shut up in that horrible place."

He went to the larder and looked inside.

" There's some milk left over here," he said, bringing out a cream-jug half full of milk. " That'll do for it to be going on with, while we think out what to do next."

Taking a saucer from the dresser, Helen filled it with milk from the jug and set it down on the floor. The kitten rushed at it and in a moment its purring filled the kitchen with such a resonance that it seemed impossible that so much sound could come from that tiny, crouching body.

Dreydel smiled. " Well, we've achieved something by our visit."

" But what do we do now ? "

" Take another look at things in the other room, I think. Then we might try asking a few questions next door. Not that people in a street like this are likely to know a single thing about their neighbours. Still, we might try."

They went back to the sitting-room.

As soon as her eyes fell again on the tray, Helen knew what it had almost reminded her of before.

" Straight gin," she said, pointing at the half-empty glass. " I've just remembered whom I've seen recently who drinks straight gin. That man Hovard who was staying at the Swan. You must have met him there."

" I'd thought of him," Dreydel said. " But he didn't strike me as the type to leave a glass with anything in it. Still, if he had other things on his mind . . ." He took a handkerchief out of his pocket, draped it over his hand then picked up the glass and sniffed its contents. His expression changed sharply. "Good God!" he murmured.

"What is it?" Helen asked.

"It isn't gin. I think . . ." He sniffed again, then cautiously dipped the tip of his little finger into the fluid and set it against his tongue. With a short laugh he put the glass back on the tray and the handkerchief into his pocket.

"Water," he said. "Plain water."

She looked at him in bewilderment.

"Well, you know your aunt and I don't," he said. "Did she drink the sherry or the water?"

"She liked sherry," Helen said, "though she'd only drink it on special occasions. But she always kept drinks in the house to offer to other people. She learnt that from Mr. Delborne."

"Did she ever drink gin?"

"I don't think so. Only sherry or port or madeira."

"What about Colliver?"

"He told me he and his sister never touch alcohol at all."

"So he might have drunk the water, though it's a queer idea to drink water out of a sherry glass. Besides, she brought the gin in for somebody she thought might want it."

"I suppose it *is* gin in the bottle," Helen said, "not water too?"

Dreydel brought out his handkerchief again, unscrewed the stopper of the bottle and sniffed.

"Unmistakably gin. And I'd be glad of some of it at the moment if I felt sure that I knew what happened in this room when it was brought out." He took a few steps across the room, stooped and picked up Mrs. Colliver's handbag. "What do you know about Hovard?"

She watched him as he opened the bag, wondering uneasily if she ought to protest at his doing so.

"Only what Bertie of the Swan told me," she said, "that he's a manufacturer of quack medicines, and that for some mysterious reason he seems to want to buy

Shipley's End. Also that he's nothing to do with Hovard and Hayle."

" What about his relations with Mrs. Andras ? "

" I don't know."

He gave her a glance. She realised, as she had done already once or twice before, how hard his face could look on occasion.

" No," she said, " I don't know. If you saw them together, you know as much as I do."

He nodded. Holding out the handbag, he said, " It seems to me there's nothing out of the ordinary in here, but would you take a look ? "

As she took the handbag from him he turned away and opened the leather writing-case that had been a present from Helen and Martin.

She was looking through the handbag, which contained, so far as she could see, only the things to be found in any woman's handbag, when she heard Dreydel catch his breath. In one of the pockets of the writing-case he had found a small packet of papers, held together by a rubber band. The band had snapped as he drew the packet out of the case and the papers had scattered over the table. He had picked one of them up and it had been what was written on it that had caused his excitement.

" I thought it must be something like that ! " he exclaimed.

" What is it ? " Helen asked.

He handed her the piece of paper.

It was a sheet of thin typing paper with a few lines written on it in blue chalk, in a large, uneven scrawl, as uncontrolled as the writing of a child. It was without punctuation or capital letters.

It read, " not the sea go away from the sea now is the time the time cannot speak to you because of the sea now the time the important time soon the secret I trust you go away from the sea."

She looked at him in astonishment.

" Whatever does it mean ? "

He handed her another sheet of paper. " See what you can make of this one."

It looked much the same as the other, except that the paper had a more crumpled appearance, as if it had been folded and unfolded more often and had spent a longer time in the writing-case.

It said, " too near you to speak the house has too many presences confusing go away you are too strong you confuse Mignon wonderfully receptive but you confuse go away I have a great deal to tell you but cannot reach you without her help me go away."

Before Helen made any comment, Dreydel handed her a third sheet of paper.

On this was written, " you are a good woman Violet you are good very you help me in my work you always helped me proof of tireless love thank thank difficult to say Mignon confused you are rare and good say nothing keep secret but write to your dear niece now she worries about you but say nothing write soon keep secret."

As she read this third message, Helen began to think that she understood what all three were about, but laying them down side by side on the table, she re-read them slowly. At first her lips silently formed the words, but as comprehension grew in her, she pressed them together in a way that made her face look as grim as Dreydel's.

Watching her, he said, " Yes—they explain a good deal, don't they ? "

" What about the rest of them ? "

" They seem to be all on the same lines, messages from the ghost of old Delborne, I suppose, to his faithful housekeeper, telling her to keep away from the house, because she confuses the medium who is his only means of communicating with her. Then for some reason he keeps ordering her to move about. It was probably when she got that first one you looked at, telling her that he couldn't speak to her because of the sea, that she decided to leave Torquay. And also at a certain point he instructed her to write to you, but not to let you into her secret—the secret that he was communicating with her and ordering her about, I should think."

" It's what's called automatic writing, isn't it ? " she said.

" It's supposed to be. But some automatic writing, I think, is at least genuinely automatic, whatever its cause may be. But this is a cold-blooded, deliberate fraud."

" But why? " Helen cried. " Why should they make her move out of the house and keep on moving about and then tell her to write to me all of a sudden? What have they to gain from that? And where is she now? And what are we going to do about it? Hadn't we better call the police? "

" And tell them what? "

" That's she's disappeared, that we can't find her, that . . . No, I suppose we can't do that yet. In spite of the slipper and all, she just might walk in at any moment. And she's been behaving so oddly for so long that it would be hard to convince them that this was different from all her other sudden moves. So what *are* we going to do? "

Dreydel collected the papers and thrust them back into the pocket of the writing-case.

" D'you know, Helen, I think you've just said something of the greatest importance. *She's been behaving oddly for so long.* . . . And who's been making her behave oddly? We know that now, don't we? The Collivers."

" But why? What have they to gain from it? "

He was still holding the writing-case and was looking down at it as if he were not sure that returning the papers to it had been the right thing to do. After a moment he took them out again. Taking his wallet from his pocket, he put the papers into the wallet, and the wallet back into his pocket, all as if it did not even occur to him that Helen might make any protest at these actions.

She was still trying to make up her mind whether or not she ought to do so when he said, " Helen, I'm now going to ask you an awkward question."

" Well? " she said.

" What do you think of me? "

Although this was a question that Helen had been asking herself intermittently for the last hour, it caught her unawares. She looked at him without in the least knowing what to say. His face was sombre and far more impersonal than the question.

"I'll explain what I mean," he said. "You see, we've walked into this situation together, each knowing very little of the other. I think—I think I can give you an explanation of the situation, but it's a very ugly one and it may occur to you that I've already worked pretty hard to sow ugly suspicions in your mind. So if you're doubtful of my motives, I think it might be best for us both if you told me so. If you think that that story I told you the other evening about the disappearance of Evelyn Lander was a fabrication for some dubious purpose of my own, or even if you think I'm simply an irresponsible crank with a bee in my bonnet—incidentally, that's what the police think, so you'd be in good company—I'd prefer not to add to the load on your mind, but just go on from here in my own way."

"I think you yourself believe that story you told me," Helen said. "I think you believe that Elvin Colliver murdered Evelyn Lander and her mother. And I think perhaps you've enough evidence to support that theory to save you from being merely a crank. But still—well, I'm not at all sure that you're right. What makes me most doubtful is just that I can't understand what motive there could be for the Collivers' treatment of my aunt. If you think you can explain that . . ."

"All right," he said. "I think I can." He walked slowly across to the fireplace, thrusting his hands into his pockets and standing there, staring down at the warm ashes. "I think this is what happened. Colliver met your aunt, who appeared to be just what he was looking for, a credulous, unprotected spinster with money. Whether she concealed from him the fact that the house and the capital weren't hers to dispose of, or whether he was in a sufficiently desperate situation to grab at marriage with her, although he knew the full facts, I don't know. But whichever it was, he and his sister soon produced a scheme to deal with the difficulty. They remembered that if a person disappears, it's seven years before they can be presumed dead. So if your aunt could be persuaded to disappear, it would be seven years, they'd reckon, before they'd have to give up the house and the money to Mrs. Andras. But a sudden disappearance would have caused questions and investigations. I don't know much about law, but I doubt somehow if they'd have been left in control of things if there was good reason to believe that Mrs. Colliver was dead. I should think at least a trustee would have been appointed to take care of things, or something like that. So the first thing they'd have to do would be to induce Mrs. Colliver to start acting in a way which would prevent too many questions being asked. And isn't that precisely what they succeeded in doing?"

"But we've all been asking questions," Helen said. "You, me, Martin, Myra . . ."

"But how much longer would you have gone on? The answer you got to your questions, the answer Colliver helped you to get by so readily giving you your aunt's address, was that she was behaving in an odd, eccentric, rather tiresome manner, but was certainly alive and apparently happy. After a little while you'd have got used to her disappearing trick, which appeared to be entirely voluntary, and you'd have stopped asking questions."

Helen nodded. "Yes."

He went on, "You were even prompted, you see, to ask those questions at the time that suited the Collivers. Mrs. Colliver, at Torquay, was given instructions to write to you, letting you have her address. But you didn't go to see her, as they hoped you would, and it was obviously an essential part of the plot that someone should go to see her. So then, I believe, they forged that letter that you accused me of having written, the letter that brought Andras down to Burnstone. That set things going as they wanted. You appeared next and then went to see your aunt. As soon as you'd done that, they made her move on again. They must have succeeded in getting complete dominion over her mind with those fake messages from old Delborne and she can't have had the least suspicion of what they were going to lead to. Colliver often went to visit her and behaved like a devoted husband. There must have been plenty of witnesses to the fact that it was she, rather than he, who was messing up the marriage. And so, when she moved once more and this time didn't supply an address, the questioning and the curiosity would soon have died down. And that's when he would have been safe to murder her, and to take her body back to Burnstone and bury it in the garden, where there's plenty of freshly dug soil now, that won't show at all where he's been doing a bit of extra digging."

Helen had been trying to interrupt before he got to the end. Now she broke in excitedly, " No, there's still something all wrong about that ! You still haven't explained *why* he should have to do all this. Or d'you think he's got such a lust for killing that he couldn't bear not to kill her, even when it wouldn't be much advantage to him ? Because he's got so little to gain by getting her out of the way—only the house and the money for a limited time, and he could have those as easily and more safely with her alive. And this scheme you've described wouldn't even help him to marry the next lonely woman with money. He can't disappear himself, taking the house and the money with him. He can't call himself a widower. No, there's something all wrong with your explanation."

" I'm sorry," Dreydel said, " there's something I've left out. I had a talk some days ago with the doctor in Burnstone, a Dr. Pepall. He didn't say much, of course, and I couldn't question him directly about his patient's affairs, but by putting two and two together I arrived at something that meets your objection and does explain why the Collivers decided to do what they did. I think that your aunt was a very sick woman. In fact, I think that she was a dying woman. Colliver may have married her, thinking that he could at least enjoy a comfortable life for a good many years, and then found out that with her heart in the state that it was, she might drop dead at any time. So the whole scheme, really, was not against her life, but was rather to induce her to die in the right place at the right time, so that her death could be concealed. You could check this by talking to Pepall yourself. He'd probably tell you more than he'd tell me."

Suddenly Helen was convinced. She sat down abruptly. Burying her face in her hands, the horror of it closed in on her, with a blackness at the edges of her vision that seemed to be spreading over her whole mind. But mercifully the darkness withdrew, like cobwebs being pulled away from her sight, and raising her head again, she looked helplessly across the small, bleak, suburban room at Dreydel.

"What do we do now?" Her voice was thin and harsh. "Even if we can't go to the police yet, if they wouldn't listen to us, we must do something. We can't just sit here and wait."

She surprised a look of contrition on his face.

"I'm a fool," he said. "I'm sorry—terribly sorry. I ought never to have poured it out like that."

"But what are we going to *do*?"

"I can only think of one thing," he said. "We could go next door and find out if there's anything they can tell us. I don't expect there will be, but it might be worth trying, while we think out what to do next."

She got wearily to her feet. A few minutes ago she had not been aware of feeling tired, but now she felt as if all her energy had been drained out of her.

"All right, let's go," she said.

They went out through the kitchen door again into the dark garden.

The house next door was a replica of the one that they had just left, but there were lights in the windows and as they approached its door, they heard some music from a radio. As soon as Dreydel rang the doorbell, quick steps came to answer it and a woman opened the door. She was about forty, with a high-coloured, friendly face, dark, waved hair and a full bosom. She had on a flowered plastic apron over a jumper and skirt. A smell of frying fish came with her to the door.

"Oh," she said in surprise, "I thought you were

Tommy," and stood there, looking at them inquiringly.
Dreydel apologised for interrupting her cooking.

"We came to see Mrs. Colliver," he said, " but she
isn't at home. Yet her back door was open, as if she'd
only gone out for a moment. So we went in and waited.
We've waited for some time, but she hasn't come back.
So—I'm sorry if it's troubling you quite uselessly—but
we wondered if you had any idea where she might have
gone."

"Mrs. Colliver?" she said. "That's the lady who's
just moved in next door into Mr. Winton's house? Mr.
Winton's gone to America for six months, something to
do with his firm, he's in hardware. I heard he was hoping
to let the house furnished and I said my niece and her
husband might like to take it, but the rent he was asking!
So they've taken a place over in Battersea, which is
nearer to his work. I like this district myself, but say
what you like, it *is* a long way up town. . . . Mrs.
Colliver, you say. That's her name?"

"Yes," Dreydel said. "You didn't see her go out by
any chance?"

"No, not unless she went away with the young gentleman," the woman said. "The one who came in the
afternoon and had such trouble getting that big trunk
into his car. I was hanging up the net curtains I'd just
washed, that's why I was at the window and saw it.
She may have been in the car for all I know. But I
don't think she was. No, come to think of it, the way
he put the trunk in, I don't think there can have been
anyone in the car. I don't care for those big trunks
myself. I'd always sooner have a couple of suitcases.
Because if you're stuck like he was with no one to help
you, where are you? Of course, he was big and strong—
and good-looking!" She gave a wide smile. "I nearly
called out I'd come and give him a hand myself, but
there I was with a lot of washing to hang out and when
I looked out of the window next he'd gone. Ever such a
good-looking boy he was, tall, dark and handsome."

"Dark?" Helen said sharply.

She was looking intently at the woman as she spoke,

ELIZABETH FERRARS

but she was aware that Dreydel turned his head and looked at her.

"That's right," the woman said. "But I don't think Mrs. Colliver was with him. She must have gone out later. Sorry I can't help. Now if you'll excuse me, that fish . . ."

"Just one moment," Dreydel said. "You didn't see anyone else come to the house before the dark young man, did you?"

She gave him an odd look, as if she had begun to find something strange in this questioning.

"No," she said brusquely. "No, I don't spend all my time keeping an eye on my neighbours. Only the young man with the big, heavy trunk."

She retreated a step and firmly closed the door.

Helen and Dreydel turned towards the gate. He made no comment whatever on the information that the woman had given them, but he put an arm round Helen's shoulders and for a moment held her close against his side.

XIII

THE KITTEN came sidling up skittishly to meet them as they came into the kitchen. It tried to have a game with them, doing complicated figures of eight around their feet, and made sudden sorties at Dreydel's shoe laces.

Absently he picked it up and started rubbing it behind its ears. But the look on his face was in sharp contrast with the gentleness of the action.

"Well, why don't you say it?" Helen said to him fiercely. "It was Martin."

"You think it was?" he said.

"Of course."

"But don't jump to conclusions," he said. "We've no evidence at all that your aunt's body was inside the trunk."

"For God's sake!" she exclaimed. "What d'you take me for? Of course it wasn't!"

110

" I thought that was what had frightened you," he said. " Wasn't it ? "

" No, it was not." But her voice, in her own ears, sounded over-emphatic. She tried to speak more calmly. " Martin's quite fond of my aunt. He was as anxious about her as I was. He told me himself; and I believed him absolutely, how glad he was to hear she was all right. Besides, Martin would never—he just couldn't——" But now, she thought, she was talking too much and too fast. She ended her sentence abruptly and almost in a mutter, as if it did not really matter what she said, " Martin couldn't do a thing like that."

Dreydel, whose hand was still rubbing the kitten's black fur behind the little pointed ears, said, " All right then, he didn't."

She was so sure that he had made up his mind that her aunt's body had been in the trunk that her look at him was full of disbelief.

He smiled sardonically. " It was your idea, you know, not mine. I'm still backing Colliver."

" But what was Martin doing here ? " she cried. " And what was in the trunk and why did he take it ? "

Dreydel tossed the kitten from him and looked down at the hands that had been holding it. They were grimy with coal-dust from its fur.

" How does your friend Andras feel about cats ? " he asked. " Does he dislike them so much that he'd shut a kitten up in a coal-shed to starve ? "

" Certainly not," she said indignantly. " He's not in the least cruel."

" Nor is Colliver—to cats. However . . ." He was smiling again, a remote, thoughtful smile, and meeting her eyes, added, " You're very much in love with him, aren't you ? "

For a moment she was quite unable to answer. Then she said simply, " I don't think so. I really don't think so."

" I think so," Dreydel said.

" I used to be," she said. " It used to be my whole life. And he still means more to me in a way than anyone I've

111

ever known. But except when we were very young, I
never had any happiness out of knowing him. That was
probably my own fault. I never could bear it that . . ."
She stopped, startled at herself. Why, of all times, should
she have chosen the present moment to start talking
about her feelings for Martin? She had never spoken
about them to anyone. They had been a very private un-
solved problem. "Anyway, Martin himself always says
that I hate him," she said. "That isn't at all true
either."

He waited without saying anything, as if he thought
that she might go on. The curious thing was that she
wanted to go on. But the chill quiet of the little house
was there to remind her as forcefully as a strident,
interrupting voice, that this was not the time for it.

"We can't just stay on like this," she said. "What
shall we do now?"

"Where does Andras live?" Dreydel asked.

"Near Regent's Park, with his mother," she answered.

"Then suppose you ring up and see if he's there. It
would help if we could get in touch with him."

"There's no telephone here," she said.

"There's a call-box in the road."

She agreed, and they went together to the call-box.

Dreydel waited outside, his shoulders hunched against
the wind, while she made the call. It was Myra who
answered.

"Helen?" she said. "Good—I'd been hoping you'd
call. What have you done with Martin, Helen? Where
is he?"

"Isn't he with you?" Helen asked.

"No, and I've seen hardly anything of him for weeks."
Myra's voice was sharp and bitter. "Ever since he went
to see you that evening, he's been behaving like a fool.
I wish to God you'd make up your mind about him—
either take him or leave him alone."

Because of the tall figure of Dreydel outside on the
pavement, possibly hearing everything she said, Helen
did her best to control the anger that began to smoulder.

"Have you seen him to-day?" she asked.

"No, I haven't seen him since . . ." Myra stopped. Helen thought she heard her speaking to someone else who was in the room with her. Then Myra went on, "I'd like to see you, Helen. I think a straight talk about one or two things might be of some use to us both. Could you come here now?"

"Not just now," Helen said. "I'm in the middle of . . . No, wait a moment. Perhaps I can." Opening the door of the call-box, she called to Dreydel and told him what had happened. "Shall I go? Even if she doesn't know where Martin is, she may have some idea why he came out here."

"Yes, I should go," he said.

"Will you come too?"

"No, I'll stay and keep an eye on things here."

Helen spoke to Myra again, saying that she would be with her in about an hour's time.

"Who's that you've just been consulting?" Myra asked suspiciously. "It isn't Martin, is it? If it is——"

"It isn't," Helen said. "I rang you up to ask if you knew where he was."

"So you say. But Martin might have told you to say that."

"Whyever should he?"

"Because he's become impossible, perfectly impossible. Nothing he says or does makes sense any more. Sometimes he seems to want to keep an eye on me all the time and sometimes he doesn't come near me for days. I've lost all patience with him."

"Tell me about it when I see you," Helen said and rang off. For a moment the thought that Myra was finding Martin impossible gave her a sense of purely malicious satisfaction, but though at any other time she might have allowed herself the luxury of dwelling on the feeling, it was quickly forgotten now.

As she stepped out of the call-box, Dreydel said, "I didn't really think he'd be there, but you may find out something. I'll ring you up to-morrow morning, and if nothing's happened either here or there, I'll go back to Burnstone and tackle Colliver. And if that leads to nothing, I'll go to the police again and *make* them listen to me."

" I'll go with you," Helen said.

" To the police ? "

" I meant to Burnstone, but to the police too, though—though, if possible I'd like to see Martin first and hear his explanation of what happened here."

He gave her another all-too-understanding look and nodded.

He walked with her towards the station but when they were near it, suddenly, without saying anything he turned and started walking rapidly back along Highfield Gardens.

Helen took the Underground to Warren Street and finished the journey in a taxi. She was very tired and felt alternately so cold and so hot that she began to wonder if she had caught a chill or was starting 'flu. Yet at the same time as she asked herself this, she knew that the chill and the fever were mostly in her mind. She tried not to think about Martin or about the interview ahead of her and what she intended to say to Myra. Oddly enough, she thought very little about her aunt either or of what could have happened to her. It was almost as if she could not think about this when she tried. Mostly she found herself thinking about Nicholas Dreydel.

At some moment in the evening she had lost the slight distrust of him that she had felt until then. When had that happened ? What had he said or done that had made it start to seem natural that he should have intruded into the affairs of herself and her aunt, that he should be questioning her about Martin and her feelings for Martin ?

She could not remember. At some point she had started to feel secure with this man whom she hardly knew, had begun to think of him as someone who was on her side in the obscure conflict in which she was becoming more and more involved. Yet she could not recall how this had come about.

The longer she thought about it, the more this lapse in her memory disturbed her. Had it been when he accepted or appeared to accept her assurance that Martin had been up to no evil with that trunk? Or when she had seen him feeding and fondling a black kitten? Or because of that deep, underlying anger in him on her aunt's account? None of these seemed to be the entire answer to her question, though all of them came near to it.

Myra Andras's smart little flat was in the attics of a big house overlooking Regent's Park. An elegant, richly carpeted staircase rose, flight after flight, past doctors' consulting rooms, until it reached the floor below Myra's. The rest of the climb was up a narrow, sharply curving stair of terrible steepness.

As Helen came panting up the last few steps, Myra appeared in the open doorway at the top.

"Now you know what keeps me slim," she said resentfully, as if the stairs were somehow Helen's fault.

She was wearing a housecoat of lime-green velvet, dark green embroidered slippers, a bracelet, on her left wrist, of heavy gold links, and long gold ear-rings that looked as if they were made of several coins strung together. Her manner was nervous and impatient and there were unusual shadows under her eyes.

"Harold's here," she said, turning and leading the way into the sitting-room. "You know Harold, don't you? . . . Harold, give Helen a drink. And give me one too while you're at it. Now, Helen . . ." She threw herself down on a low sofa, curled her feet under her and threw her head back against a cushion, staring up at Helen with bitter anger in her dark, tired eyes. "I'm not going to beat about the bush. I've known you far too long for that. I insist on your telling me straight out, what have you been doing to Martin?"

From a deep armchair on the opposite side of the fireplace, Harold Hovard had risen to his feet.

"Not so fast, not so fast, the little lady's frozen cold," he said, holding out a large warm hand to Helen. "Cold night, eh? Why, your poor little hand's like ice. Come and sit down here, my dear, and don't let Myra bother you about that precious son of hers till you've got nice and warm and got a nice strong drink inside you."

"Well, while you're being so protective, don't go

breathing your germs all over her," Myra snapped. " Would you believe it, Helen, he's got an awful cold and he's trying to cure it with one of his own wretched quack medicines. There's touching faith for you. Nothing will cure a cold, nothing! But no wonder he can sell the frightful things to other people if he can sell them to himself."

" It isn't a cold, it's just a slight catarrh," Hovard said touchily. " You'll see, it'll be gone by to-morrow. I'll take another couple of my tablets to-night with a nice glass of hot whisky and water and to-morrow there won't be a thing the matter with me. Now what'll you have to drink, Miss Gamlen ? What about a nice pink gin ? "

" Thank you." Helen dropped into the chair by the fire. It occurred to her that she had not eaten since midday and that it was perhaps foolish of her to accept a drink, yet she wanted it badly.

Hovard stooped over the tray of bottles and glasses. Though he was not a tall man, Myra's smallness and delicacy seemed to confer on him a lumbering, bear-like size, so that he seemed to take up too much space in the low-ceilinged, charming room. He had to interrupt himself in the middle of mixing the drinks to blow his nose heavily into a large, gaily coloured handkerchief. His eyes were red and watery and his voice was thick.

As he brought Helen her gin, Myra started speaking again, stabbing the air as she did so with a cigarette that she had taken up but had not lit.

" I don't want to be unreasonable, Helen. I don't want you to think that I'm trying to step between you and Martin. Heaven knows, he's old enough to make up his own mind about such things by now, and so are you. But I do object to this cat and mouse game you play with him. You know what he's like, he's so devilishly highly strung and temperamental that it makes him quite desperate. And that's no fun for me. For weeks now I haven't known when he was going to walk in and when he was going to disappear for days on end. And when he has been around, his temper's been past bearing."

Helen took a sip of her gin.

" Well ? " she said.

" Well ! " Myra exploded. " Is that all you've got to say ? "

" If you imagine," Helen said, " that Martin's been spending his time with me, you're quite wrong."

" Where has he been, then ? "

" Some of the time recently he's been at Burnstone."

Helen saw Myra and Hovard exchange a glance.

When Myra went on, there was something defensive in her tone, as if she were arguing against some conviction of her own. " Whatever should he be doing in Burnstone ? "

" Still trying to find out if my aunt's alive, or——" Helen had started to speak in a hard, almost flippant tone, but suddenly she could not go on. Putting her glass down quickly, she put her hands over her eyes. The sense of the darkness closing in was there again.

His voice sounding remote and dim, she heard Hovard say, " Look at that now. The little lady's quite upset."

" Give her one of your pills or powders then, Harold," Myra said with a short laugh. " Surely you've got something that'll put her right in two ticks."

The laugh made Helen pull herself together. She raised her head and reached for her glass.

" That's right—that's the best medicine," Hovard said. His ruddy face, blotched and puffy-looking with his cold, looked genuinely concerned. " What's the trouble, my dear ? I know Myra's a hell of a little bully when she's got one of her moods on, but you're too tough to let that get you down. Something's wrong, isn't it ? Go on, tell us about it."

" I want to know something first," Helen said. " When did you last see Martin, Myra ? "

" Days ago," Myra said. " Almost a week ago."

" Did he tell you anything about my aunt then—that he knew where she was, or anything like that ? "

" God, if you knew how fed up I am with that imbecile aunt of yours ! " Myra exclaimed. She sprang to her feet. " No, we never mentioned your aunt. Strangely enough, we spend very little of our time talking about

117

your aunt. Your aunt, as a topic of conversation, has been exhausted."

" Then you don't know that she's been living in Barnet for the last two or three weeks and that Martin's been to visit her there ? " Helen said.

" She's in Barnet ? " Myra said. " Well, why not ? Have you come to tell me I ought to have called on her ? "

" Just a moment," Hovard said. He leant towards Helen. " You've got something more to tell us. You didn't nearly throw a faint just because your boy-friend's been visiting your aunt in Barnet. Come on now, what's the real trouble ? "

" It's just that she isn't there any more," Helen said. " She's gone—vanished again—at least, it looks like it. I was out there earlier this evening with Mr. Dreydel, and there wasn't a sign of her. But the back door had been left open, and her handbag was in the sitting-room . . ."

She told the rest of it quickly. She told them about the slipper, about the kitten locked up in the coal-shed, about the notes in the writing-case. She told them also that a neighbour had seen Martin come to that house that afternoon. But she did not offer them Dreydel's explanation of the notes and her aunt's curious behaviour during the past year. Nor did she mention the trunk that Martin had taken from the house.

She held their attention, but their reactions to her story were very different. Hovard, blowing his nose and mopping his watering eyes, seemed to take it seriously. When she finished, he said nothing for a moment, then said, " This man Dreydel—where does he fit into all this ? "

Myra had sat down again on the sofa, with her elbows on her knees, her chin on her hands, her eyes full of distrust and a hard little smile on her lips. She spoke at the same time as Hovard. " So Martin is to be produced as a witness of all this, is he ? You've involved him in it somehow."

Helen chose to answer Myra. " You don't believe what I've told you ? "

" I don't know," Myra said. " I really don't know. I've always taken for granted you were perfectly honest— you and Miss Gamlen. But now I can't help wondering."

" Hush now, hush ! " Hovard said. " That's a shocking thing to say, my dear. You'll be hurting our little friend's feelings and she'll get up and go before we've had a chance to get to the bottom of all this—and who's to blame her ? Now, my dear . . ." This was to Helen again. " Tell us about this man Dreydel. He's been staying at Burnstone, hasn't he ? I've had several drinks with him. I liked him. Good straightforward type, I thought. But all the same, where does he come in ? "

" Isn't it obvious ? " Myra said. " I don't pretend I understand what the racket is, but they're all in it together, the Collivers and the Gamlens and now this man too, who's the reason, I suppose, why Helen's been treating Martin as she has. Well, that's her affair. I never wanted her and Martin to marry and I always wished he'd make up his mind to get her out of his system. I always told him she was ambitious and cal- culating and not to be relied on, but he'd never really look at any other woman but her. So if he sees now with his own eyes that he isn't the only man she ever thinks about, it'll be a damn' good thing ! "

" Now, now, you're to stop this, Myra," Hovard said. " You're saying a lot of mighty unpleasant things that you're going to regret terribly. You don't really mean them. This isn't you at all."

To Helen's surprise, Myra flushed and dropped her eyes.

" Yes," she said. " I suppose so. I'm sorry, Helen. I really don't know what I'm saying."

Perhaps it was because of her tiredness or the load of all the other things that she had on her mind, but Myra's accusations had hardly touched Helen.

Myra went on, " I know he really loves you, Helen. He's played around a lot with other girls, but none of them mattered much. I'm probably the person who's most to blame for all the troubles you had with him.

I've been so damn' lonely myself, I got much too possessive. But I never meant to make trouble. Why don't you forget it ? "

Helen stood up. Like her anger, her surprise at this speech of Myra's was far less than she would have expected. Again her tiredness and her worries and perhaps the gin too, seemed to have raised a cloud between her and the other two people in the room.

" Well, if Martin telephones again or comes to see you," she said, " will you tell him I want to see him—that it's urgent ? "

She went to the door.

Myra followed her.

" Helen, listen to me," she said. " Martin loves you."

" I don't really think so," Helen said.

" He doesn't believe you love him, but I think you do. Don't you ? "

" Tell him to ring me up," Helen said. " Tell him I've got to speak to him."

She started down the steep little stair. Though she did not look back, she knew that Myra did not move, but stood there watching her until she was out of sight.

Helen took a taxi home and because she was far too tired to cook, made herself a thick sandwich with some cold meat that was in the refrigerator and opened a tin of soup. Putting these things on a tray and taking the tray into the sitting-room, she sat down on the hearthrug close to the gas-fire, and until she had got rid of her hunger and had started on a cigarette, stayed, almost voluntarily, in her dazed and thoughtless state. But at last, fed, warmed and a little rested, she sent her thoughts back to her interview with Myra and found herself thinking, more than anything else, of the fact that Harold Hovard had been wearing slippers.

Several things made sense now, she thought. For if Hovard were Myra's lover, that alone would explain much of Martin's recent behaviour. He would hate Hovard, he would hate his presence in their home, he would be as jealously possessive towards his mother as she had ever been towards him. And in such a mood, the person to whom he would naturally turn would be Helen, partly because this would anger his mother more than anything else he could do, and partly because, among such women as he might know, Helen was the one whom he could most nearly put in his mother's place.

Remembering how he had told her that he had troubles on his mind, that he had wanted badly to talk to her, but that she made it too difficult for him, she thought now that she could say for certain that those troubles of his were all connected with Harold Hovard.

But now Myra actually wanted her son to marry Helen, or said that she did.

This might be genuine, because Martin had made himself too troublesome to her, distracting her and upsetting her love-affair, or it might be because Hovard had enough power over her emotions to be able to dictate it to her.

Helen thought about Hovard. He was not the sort of man by whom she would have expected Myra to be attracted, for Myra, apart from anything else, was a snob. But he had a strong personality, a strong will and would always know, calmly and probably selfishly, what he wanted. In sheer contrast to her over-sensitive son, this might have a great fascination for her. She might even be thinking of marrying him.

And that, Helen thought drowsily, letting her head fall back against the chair behind her, might explain Myra's sudden interest in Shipley's End. For to do her justice, Myra had never shown herself greedy until now. In saying that she was glad that Mrs. Colliver had had a reward for her years of service, she had seemed to be sufficiently sincere. But if Harold Hovard had got it into his head that the house and the money at present being enjoyed by an ex-housekeeper could somehow be acquired by Myra, he might take a more active interest in the idea of marriage with her than would be the case if her present moderate income were all that she had to offer.

Helen's eyes closed. She told herself that she had

better get into bed straight away, before she fell asleep here by the fire. But she still did not know what Martin had been doing at 11 Highfield Gardens with that big trunk.

XIV

IN THE MORNING, as she was having her breakfast, Dreydel telephoned. He told her that he had waited at the house until late in the evening, then had gone to a hotel for the night and returned in the early morning to the house. But there was still no sign of Mrs. Colliver, or of anyone else having been there.

" So I've locked up," he said, " and I'm going back to Burnstone to see Colliver. Are you coming too ? "

" Yes," Helen said. " I'll meet you at Paddington."

" What about your work ? "

" I expect I can get a day or two off if I tell them I've got serious family trouble."

" All right then," he said. " At Paddington, at the booking-office in about an hour's time."

He rang off.

Helen swallowed another cup of coffee, telephoned the art-school, thrust a few things into her little overnight case, left the washing-up to be done on her return and set off for the station.

Dreydel was already there when she reached it. He was carrying a square cardboard box, tied up with string.

" There's a train in a few minutes," he said. " We'd better try to catch it. Did you have any luck last night ? "

" I didn't find Martin, if that's what you mean," she said. " He hasn't been home much lately and Myra didn't know where he was. But I did find something out."

" So did I," he said, " but let's save it till we're in the train."

They hurried through the barrier and got on to the

train just as the porters were beginning to slam the doors. But the train was half-empty and they had no difficulty in finding a compartment to themselves.

As soon as they had settled themselves, Helen started on a description of her visit to Myra. She told Dreydel of her belief that Hovard was Myra's lover and of how this had probably affected Martin.

He nodded from time to time and when she had finished, stayed silent for a moment, thinking it over. There was an increased restlessness about him this morning, as if he were repressing some strong excitement. At the same time he looked rather more unkempt than usual, and as if he had not slept much.

He had put the cardboard box on the seat beside him. It had several holes punched in its lid and Helen, glancing at it, thought she saw something stir inside it.

" What is it ? " she asked.

" That ? Oh, the kitten," he said. " Couldn't leave it to starve and I didn't want to ask the woman next door to look after it, after asking her all those questions yesterday. Besides, I've had an idea . . ." But he stopped there, frowning, looking as if he were trying to recapture a thought that Helen's question had driven out of his mind. After an instant he went on, " You believe then that Andras would be against his mother marrying ? "

" He'd be against her marrying Harold Hovard," Helen said. " He's the sort of man who'd grate on every scrap of sensibility that Martin possesses."

" And you think that the marriage is more likely to happen if Mrs. Andras can get hold of the house and the money than if she can't, and that therefore young Andras couldn't possibly wish any harm to your aunt."

" Yes," Helen said, " that is what I think."

" I'm not arguing against the idea," he said slowly, " but hasn't it struck you that you could put it the other way round ? Suppose Mrs. Andras was the one who was marrying for money. Suppose her wish to marry Hovard, if she does wish to marry him, is simply for the sake of the income that he makes out of his quack medicines. Then her son might desperately try to save her from this by—well, that's to say——"

" Go on, say it ! " Helen said furiously.

To her astonishment, he began to laugh. Though this only increased her anger, it occurred to her unexpectedly how seldom she had seen him laugh and how his face changed when it happened.

" I'm sorry," he said, " there isn't really a joke."

" I didn't think there was," she said.

" Putting me down as a hysterical type, who laughs without reason," he suggested. " I was just wondering how long it's going to take you to come to terms with yourself about Andras."

" Listen," she said, " for some reason everyone's suddenly taken to trying to sell me Martin. Well, I know Martin, I'm very fond of him and I don't think he's a murderer. I can think that without being in love with him, can't I ? "

" I'd like to think so, since I think I'm beginning to fall in love with you myself," he said. " But going back to what we were talking about . . ."

For an instant Helen could not think what on earth they had been talking about. She looked at him blankly and a little wildly. He started laughing again.

" I wish you wouldn't," she said uneasily.

" Wouldn't laugh or wouldn't talk ? " he said. " I'm not sure I can help myself in either case. My trouble is, I had a sleepless night and did too much unbalanced thinking. I began to find wonderful possibilities in casting your Martin as a murderer. But there's still Colliver, you see—the man who never says die when it comes to murder —and always says die to his wives. I'm still backing Colliver, though I'm sure when we get to Burnstone, we'll find he's got a perfectly impregnable alibi. And that brings me round to what I wanted to tell you about the milk. You remember the bottle of milk in the kitchen ? "

" Yes."

" Well, I saw the milkman this morning. He delivers about eight o'clock. He told me that he delivered as usual yesterday morning and that he saw Mrs. Colliver.

She took the bottle from him, paid his bill and chatted to him for a few minutes and said nothing whatever about going away and wanting the delivery discontinued."

"So whatever happened, happened during yesterday and not during the night before."

"And she was not expecting to make one of her sudden moves."

"And you believe that Elvin Colliver will have some sort of perfect alibi for the whole of yesterday?"

"I'm sure he will."

"But suppose the alibi *is* perfect?"

"We'll then have to consider whether it was really Mrs. Colliver whom the milkman saw—whether, in fact, it's been Mrs. Colliver at all at 11 Highfield Gardens."

She turned away from him, looking out of the window. There was a little blue in the sky, but the leafless suburbs looked drearily lost in winter.

"There's just one thing I'd thought of," she said, "one thing against the Collivers having had anything to do with it. . . . That automatic writing. The notes in the writing-case. If they'd done a murder or—or anything—would the Collivers ever have risked leaving those behind? I know that makes it sound as if I'm thinking of Martin, but I'm not. He's an egotistical and very irresponsible person, he does crazy things and lives half the time in a world of preposterous fantasy. Yet he's very intelligent and sometimes quite selfless." She paused. "I don't suppose that makes sense."

"People don't have to make sense," Dreydel said.

"Oh, they do—when you know enough about them, they do, and when we find out what he was doing with that trunk, it'll make sense, it won't be anything impossible and incredible like a murder. So I'm not really worried about him, in spite of those notes."

He nodded, but again said nothing. What she had said seemed to have given him something to think about, for now he turned away, looking out of the window.

At Oxford they changed into the Burnstone bus, reaching the bus-stop opposite the Old Swan soon after mid-day. There was a glitter of sunshine on the front of the old building and the sky had been growing bluer, yet the day was not like the soft and golden autumn day, a few weeks ago, on which Helen, for the first time after a long interval, had come to Burnstone and with surprise rediscovered its beauty.

To-day the air was cold, the sunshine had a sharp, astringent quality and the fallen leaves in the ditches, those that had not vanished away on the wind or been trodden into the mud, had lost their varied colours and changed into the uniform black of death and winter.

Helen and Dreydel had decided to go straight to Shipley's End, but in the car-park outside the Swan, Dreydel caught sight of a smart, light blue Sunbeam Talbot and pointing at it, said, " That's Hovard's."

" So he's back again," Helen said. " I wonder if Myra's with him. "

" It might be a good thing to find out," Dreydel said, " and if possible, what's brought them. They may have come to the same conclusion, thinking over what you told them, as we did."

" As you did," Helen said as they went towards the Swan.

They found Myra and Hovard in the bar. Myra looked irritated when she saw them and gave Dreydel a questioning, antagonistic stare, but Hovard called out to them cheerfully, asking them what they would have to drink. He, as usual, was drinking straight gin, Myra a Martini.

" Thought somehow we might see you here," he said. " We took a run out to Barnet first thing this morning, but found the house there all shut up, so then we came on down here. The little lady wants to have things out with the Collivers—says she means to go to the police if they don't produce Mrs. Colliver. I don't know what you think about that, eh ? " He cocked a bushy dark eyebrow at Helen.

In a surprised tone she said, " Your cold really is better."

He laughed boisterously, slapped his knee and said, " Didn't I tell you ? Look, I don't usually mix business and pleasure, and I don't go in for advertising to my friends, but those pills of mine really are the goods. You saw me last night and you see me to-day—well, you could hardly have a better proof of it, could you?" He laid a large hand on Helen's shoulder and left it there. "You know, my dear, people jeer at people like me because we haven't got a lot of letters after our names, but there are plenty of things simple folk know that are shrouded in mystery, utter mystery, to all the clever people. And all I've ever done is get hold of a little of that simple, primitive knowledge and put it up in bottles and sell it. And what's wrong with doing that? I've helped a lot of people through it."

"For God's sake!" Myra said. "You and the Collivers, you're all of a piece."

"Well, I won't argue that," he said. "People like them, they help other people too. And who's to say what's genuine and what's fake in what they do? 'There are more things in heaven and earth, Horatio . . .'"

Myra put her hands over her ears. "I knew you'd say that! I knew it, I knew it!"

Dreydel, who had been fiddling with the knots in the string round his cardboard box, removed the lid, lifted out the black kitten and set it down on the bar. It looked round in a dazed fashion, miaowing once or twice, stretched itself lengthily, extending all its claws, then settled down contentedly to clean itself.

Myra and Hovard both stared at the kitten as if the sight of it hypnotised them. They seemed as astonished by its appearance as they might have been if Dreydel had produced, not one kitten out of a cardboard box, but a dozen white rabbits out of a top hat.

"Really," Myra said, looking at last from the kitten to Dreydel, "you are a perfectly amazing person. Does this kitten accompany you wherever you go?"

"Only since last night," Dreydel said. "I'm taking it home to Mignon Colliver. I fancy it's her property."

"Which reminds me," Hovard said, "before we go to see those people, I want to phone my lawyer. I've had a little experience of the sort of things this little lady can say when she starts to shoot her mouth off and I want to ask him a thing or two about slander and so on and also where she'll be if she insists on going to the police. I'm not a person who goes looking for trouble and I like to be on the safe side when it comes. So if you'll excuse me . . ."

He hurried out.

Myra seemed surprised. "The things *I* say . . .? Well, he scares easily, doesn't he? Much more easily than you, Helen. But perhaps he's right. Perhaps I really am a dangerous sort of bitch." She looked quite put out at the thought. "I've a lot of things on my mind," she added.

Like Martin, Helen thought, when he had last come to see her. He had had a lot of things on his mind.

"You haven't seen Martin yet, I suppose," she said.

"No, but what's the good of worrying?" Myra said. "He's grown up, isn't he? Or isn't he? Perhaps you know more about that than I do. But I'll tell you something about him which I didn't want to tell you while Harold was here. Harold and Martin, you see—they don't get on too well. You wouldn't expect them to, would you, though Harold, in his rather awful way, has really done his best. It's been quite funny to watch sometimes. Still, what I meant to tell you is this. I did know your aunt was living at Barnet. Martin rang up and told me that she was and that he'd seen her. That was several days ago. I think he did it because of the things I'd said to you about the way she disappeared if someone who might recognise her—other than you, I mean—tried to see her. So I'm very sorry about that, Helen. Of course I didn't seriously suspect you, it's just that I felt sure something damn fishy was going on and I didn't know *whom* to blame. And I really am sorry. And then yesterday afternoon Martin rang me up and said I wasn't to tell anyone he'd told me where Miss Gamlen was, or that I knew anything about her at all, and he sounded so strange and excited that—well, I've been worrying myself sick ever since, wondering what trouble he's got himself into. And that's really why I've come down here. I'm going to see the Collivers and put the fear of death into them somehow, till I find out what's going on."

"Why don't you come with us now?" Dreydel said. "We're going to see them."

Myra considered it. "Perhaps I will. But what about Harold?"

"Bring him along too, if you like."

But Harold Hovard, whom they found at the telephone, seemed remarkably glad that Myra had found someone else to accompany her on her visit to the Collivers. As she turned towards the door, Hovard caught Helen's eye and gave her a wink. Following Myra, Helen reflected that if these two oddly assorted middle-aged people were in love with one another and contemplating marriage, it was at least without illusions.

As they walked towards Shipley's End, she wondered what the impulse had been that had made Dreydel invite Myra to join them. He had put the kitten back in its box and had the box under his arm. After its taste of freedom in the bar it seemed to resent this treatment, keeping up a high, complaining crying nearly all the way, a sound almost as piteous as that which had attracted their attention to the coal-shed.

The noise got on Myra's nerves. Fretfully she demanded that Dreydel should take the creature out of its box and carry it under his arm.

"Or let me carry it," she said. "Anything to stop that awful keening. It's killing me."

"Keening?" Dreydel said. "That's what's done for the dead, isn't it?"

"Now just why need you say a thing like that?" she exclaimed.

"Sorry," he said, "it's on my mind."

"You and Helen believe that Miss Gamlen's dead, don't you?"

When neither of them answered she gave a laugh.

"Now I think I know why I've been included in the party," she said. "You want me to make all the indiscreet accusations for you. Well, I'm not going to. I shall stay in the background and see how you handle things. That'll be interesting."

" It probably will," Dreydel agreed.

" Anyway, give me that kitten to hold," she insisted.

He took the lid off the box and let Myra lift the kitten out. She was holding it in her arms, rubbing it gently under its chin and giving it the tip of its own tail to play with to keep it quiet, when they reached Shipley's End. When Elvin Colliver opened the door to them, it was only the kitten that he appeared to see. He looked at it first with surprise, then with great astonishment.

" Good gracious me," he said, " I do believe that's little Bess." He looked closer. " Yes, it is, I'm sure it is. That little spot on her nose . . ." At last he looked at the three people on his threshold. " But what an extraordinary thing. Wherever did you find her ? Or am I all wrong ? It is Bess, isn't it ? "

" Well, take her, take her," Myra said, " if you know her so well. And then please ask us to come in, Mr. Colliver. These two people, Helen and Mr. Dreydel, have something important to say to you."

" I'm so sorry," Colliver said apologetically, still unable to take his eyes off the kitten. " But I can't get over suddenly seeing Bess like this. Did you find her in the road or the garden ? They say a cat will always find its way home again, however carefully you keep it shut up on the journey, but a little kitten like that . . .! Where did you find it ? "

" Locked up in the coal-shed at 11 Highfield Gardens," Dreydel answered.

Colliver started. He looked swiftly from Dreydel's face to Helen's. " Oh, so you've been to Barnet," he said.

He said it in a tone that puzzled Helen. It was not frightened, it was not angry. It was sad, disappointed and rather irritated. Giving a sharp little sigh, he added, " Well, come in," and turning, led the way to the drawing-room. Their information appeared to have shocked his usual effusiveness out of him, and given him something to think about, yet had had less effect somehow than might have been expected.

Going into the house, Myra looked about her with unconcealed disgust, wrinkling up her nose at the smell of damp, of cats and of unaired neglect. Mignon was in the drawing-room. She was sitting on the floor near the fire, which was a little larger and less smoky than Helen had seen it before. The tortoiseshell cat that had sprung at Helen in the garden on her first visit lay across Mignon's lap, and two others, their sinuous bodies entwined, lay on the hearth-rug near her. She was reading, holding the page close to her eyes.

Like her brother, she at first showed far more interest in the black kitten than in her visitors. He told her hurriedly, so hurriedly that it was almost as if it were to prevent her asking questions in front of the others, that the kitten was Bess and that it had been brought from Barnet.

" Though I don't yet know why it's been brought back to us," he said. He looked at Dreydel. " I suppose there was a reason."

" We didn't know what else to do with it," Dreydel said, " since we didn't like to think of it starving to death."

" But surely Violet—my wife—I mean to say, she was so fond of it," Colliver said. " She was so pleased with it when I brought it to her. Did she ask you to bring it back to us ? "

" We didn't see her," Dreydel said. " The house was empty and the kitten was locked up in the coal-shed."

" Locked up in the . . .? "

" Wait, Elvin ! " Mignon had fastened the clair-voyant stare of her grey, glassy eyes on Dreydel. Her fuzzy, murmuring voice spoke with unusual authority. " I can see that something serious has happened. These people have not come here merely to bring us a kitten. They have come to bring us news. Bad news, I think. Don't ask me how I know that. I know it and I ask you to prepare yourself. Now, Mr. Dreydel."

Dreydel answered with a kind of diffidence. " Yester-day Miss Gamlen and I went to see Mrs. Colliver. But there seemed to be no one at home and we should have come away again. if we hadn't heard the back door banging in the wind. That seemed to us rather surprising. Miss Gamlen didn't think her aunt would have gone out, leaving the door unlocked, and was afraid that perhaps she was at home but had been taken ill and couldn't come to the door. So we went in and found the house empty. There were several things, however, that we couldn't understand." He described then what he and Helen had found that had roused their anxiety, but made no suggestions of any kind as to the possible meaning of these things. He ended by telling how they had discovered the kitten.

Colliver's forehead looked damp. He passed a hand across it.

" But surely—surely Violet came back later," he said. " She'd gone for a little walk—she liked to do that—or to the cinema."

" No," Mignon said in the voice that without being raised at all could sound so decided. " She didn't come back. I know."

" No," Dreydel said, " she didn't. Miss Gamlen went away but I came back again later in the evening and again next morning and there was still no sign of Mrs. Colliver."

" And we still haven't been told," Myra said, looking at him sharply, " where you come into all this, Mr. Dreydel. The whole situation is fishy in the extreme, and you're by no means the least fishy part of it."

Both Dreydel and Colliver acted as if they had not heard this. Helen knew that something had happened between the two men, that some message had been passed from one to the other and perhaps even been answered, and that in reality both of them were now almost unaware of the presence of anyone else in the room.

" But I saw Violet only the day before yesterday," Colliver said, not looking directly at Dreydel, yet speaking only to him. " I took her the kitten and she seemed so pleased with it. I stayed till quite late, coming back on the midnight train. We had a very happy evening together and she said nothing at all about going away."

" If you took that train," Dreydel said, " how did you

get from Oxford to Burnstone? There aren't any buses at that time of night."

" I'd ordered a car," Colliver said, " from Morrison's Garage."

" And to-day ? " Dreydel said.

" What about to-day ? "

" Where have you been all day ? "

" Why, here, of course. Out in the garden most of the time. To my great surprise, I'm actually beginning to enjoy gardening and though it's been cold to-day, it was nice and dry. . . . Why are you asking me these questions ? "

Myra answered, " He's asking you for your alibi, Mr. Colliver—as if you didn't know that ! And you have one all nice and ready, I see—a hired car from a local garage, so you can easily prove you did get home on the midnight train—and then a day spent in the garden, where half the inhabitants of the village will have seen you. Well, Mr. Dreydel, what next ? "

" Mrs. Andras," he said, " I was under the impression that you intended to stay in the background."

" That's what I'm doing—that's to say, I'm just being a kind of Greek chorus, explaining and helping things along," she said. " Mr. Colliver *has* got a nice alibi, hasn't he ? "

" But is this the truth ? " Colliver exclaimed. " Do you really believe some harm has come to my wife and that I—I, of all people !—may have had something to do with it ? "

" Yes," Mignon Colliver said. " That is what he thinks. I knew it, I could feel it, as soon as he came to the house. But I don't blame him, in fact, I feel grateful to him. It isn't important what he thinks about you or me, Elvin. What is important is that he cares enough about poor Violet to come here and say these things."

" Thank you, Miss Colliver," Dreydel said. " I was sure you'd understand me. I'm very much concerned about Mrs. Colliver, because I can't believe, considering the evidence, that she left that house voluntarily. And

I've been wanting to make an appeal to you to help me find her."

" An appeal—to me ? " Mignon said.

" Yes, I thought that with your powers, your gift . . ."

" I'm going to the police ! " Colliver said in a suddenly loud voice.

" Wait, Elvin," his sister said. " What do you mean, Mr. Dreydel ? "

" Well, aren't there—I don't know how to put this— aren't there powers from whom, through you, we might be able to get guidance of some sort ? "

She looked at him incredulously. Then she looked scared. The bony little hand that until then had been smoothing the fur of the tortoiseshell cat, fluttered up to her mouth.

" Oh no, oh no," she said, " don't ask that. You don't know what you're asking."

" This is a case for the police," her brother said. " I'll telephone—no, I'll go and see them—at once."

" Please, Miss Colliver," Dreydel said.

" But don't you see, I never, never *ask* for anything," she said. " That isn't my way and I don't know what would happen if I tried it. I'm simply receptive. I let the power, as you call it, come to me and pass through me. I'd be frightened, truly frightened, of asking for anything."

" Couldn't we do the asking ? " Dreydel said.

Myra giggled.

It was unlikely, Helen thought, that she intended this to be helpful, yet its effect on Mignon Colliver was to bring a gleam into her pale eyes and to make her jerk her head up.

" The suggestion," she said sternly to Myra, " is not at all ridiculous. I have no confidence in the success of such an attempt, but that's because I have no confidence in myself, because I know my own unworthiness and inadequacy. But if Mr. Dreydel has confidence in me and desires me to do this——"

" Mignon ! " her brother said. " I'm going to the police. Don't you think that's what I ought to do ? "

But he was too late now to check his sister. Myra's laughter had fanned the small flame lit by Dreydel and Mignon had become determined to show them what she could do.

Helen at first could not understand Dreydel's motive. She wondered at his wasting time just then in inducing Mignon to give a seance, for even if she were to reveal herself as an obvious fraud, this would not be of much help now in finding Mrs. Colliver. Then Helen realised that he might merely be trying to obtain a specimen of Mignon's supposedly automatic writing, to compare with the messages that they had found in the writing-case.

Mignon told her brother to arrange some chairs in a semi-circle, then herself sat down in an arm-chair with a small coffee-table at her side. On the coffee-table she placed several sheets of plain typing paper, then let her right hand, holding a blue chalk, rest limply on the paper.

"And we'll have the curtains drawn and perhaps a little music just to begin with," she said. "That isn't always necessary, but this isn't—well, it isn't a really sympathetic atmosphere, I'm afraid, and I may need a little help." As her brother went to draw the fine though shabby damask curtains, she looked piercingly at Dreydel and ail, "You understand I guarantee nothing."

He nodded gravely.

With the curtains drawn the room was not really dark, for the fire was burning quite brightly and after the first moment Helen found it was easy to see the faces of the other people there, as well as Mignon's hand lying on the blank sheet of paper. She saw Elvin turning over some gramophone records, choosing one and putting it on the gramophone. She saw the mocking grin of Myra's face, as well as hearing her giggle again, when the music that he had chosen turned out to be "Jesu, joy of man's desiring."

"Quiet now, please," Elvin said, playing his role of stage-manager, though obviously unwillingly.

"But is this all?" Myra said. "Do we just sit here like this?"

"Of course we could put on more of a show for you,

if you like," he answered ironically. "We could start tables rapping and have mysterious manifestations and all sorts of things. I'll admit that occasionally, because the customers insisted on it, we've done that sort of thing. But if you want the simple and true thing, here it is." He took his place on one of the chairs, facing Mignon and between Myra and Helen.

When the record came to an end, he rose softly and changed it. Mignon made no movement of any kind, except that after a little while her head lolled a little to one side and her eyes closed. When the second record ended, Colliver did not replace it but stayed very still, leaning forward, his eyes, reflecting the firelight, fixed intently on his sister's face.

Helen had no idea how long they sat there in the darkened room before Mignon's hand began to move. Its movement was sudden and in no way like writing, for it simply travelled straight across the piece of paper. Even in the firelight, Helen could see the thick, dark line the blue pencil had made. Then came a lot of meaningless meandering. When the paper was half-covered with scrawls, Elvin rose softly and slipped it out from under Mignon's hand, leaving her a clean sheet to work on. The scrawling went on till a second piece of paper had been covered by it and then removed by Elvin.

It was not until she reached the fourth sheet that Mignon began to write what looked to Helen, seated several feet away, like some words. She wrote one line, then her hand rose sharply in the air and started to tremble violently. The blue pencil fell out of her fingers. A tremor ran through her body and she sat up.

"Well?" she said in her normal voice, sounding only moderately interested in what might have happened.

Elvin moved to pick up the sheet of paper, but Dreydel reached it first. Going over to the window and pulling the curtains back, he read the message written in the same hand as those that Helen had seen in the house in Barnet. He looked utterly bewildered at what he read. His lips moved, as if he were saying it over to himself to see if it made better sense that way. Then he held it out to Mignon.

"Perhaps you can explain it," he said.

She looked at it, apparently as unaware of what was written there as the others in the room. As she read it, a violent spasm gripped her features. Her eyes seemed to start out of her head. She gave a scream and fainted.

As the paper fluttered out of her hand, Helen saw what was written on it.

"She is with evelyn lander."

XV

WALKING BACK to the Swan, Myra said, " I'd very much like to know what all that was about."

"So would I," Dreydel said.

She gave him a sidelong look. "As if you didn't." She turned to Helen. "You know what it was all about, I suppose." But just then they came in sight of the Swan and she exclaimed, "There's our car! That means Martin's come. Now what's he done that for?" She quickened her steps.

As Dreydel and Helen let her draw ahead of them, Helen asked in a low voice, "What *was* it all about? When you started setting the scene, getting Mignon to give a demonstration, I thought you were simply checking the handwriting of those messages we found. Incidentally, what was the message that Mignon did write this time— the one you palmed when you substituted the one about Evelyn Lander?"

He put a hand into his pocket and brought out a crumpled piece of paper. "It wasn't very interesting or original, I'm afraid," he said. "She was playing safe."

There, in the familiar blue scrawl, were the words, "I am the resurrection and the life."

"Well, you ought to be satisfied with the success of your experiment," Helen said.

"Yes, I got more of a reaction even than I'd hoped."

But he did not look satisfied. There was an uncertainty on his face that Helen had not seen before.

" What is it ? " she asked. " What's gone wrong ? "

He stood still. Ahead of them, Myra had just turned in at the door of the Swan.

" I don't know," he said. " It's just a feeling I've got. . . . I think something's gone wrong in the Collivers' plans. There was something in the way Colliver behaved. He was upset, depressed, despondent, but not scared. Or was he just hiding it very well ? " While he spoke, he was frowning in an absent way at the Andras's car, parked at the side of the road near the entrance to the Swan. " Look, I rather want to think this over," he went on. " D'you mind if I don't come in with you now ? I think best when I'm walking."

Helen gave a nod but she did not go on towards the hotel.

" Nicholas," she began, but realising that she had just unthinkingly used his first name and that he too had been instantly aware of this fact, she momentarily could not remember what she had intended to say. " When will you come back ? " she asked, instead of whatever it was that had slipped out of her mind.

" I don't quite know," he said.

" But you've had no lunch yet."

" It doesn't matter. Go in and have yours. I'll get some bread and cheese somewhere if I need it."

" All right." She went on towards the doorway of the Swan.

As soon as she had separated from him, she knew what it was that she had wanted to ask him. She had wanted to ask what he thought about Elvin's alibi. He had told her to expect an alibi, and she had wanted to know if the one that had been offered had been less assailable than he had expected.

Perhaps, she thought, going into the hotel, that was the problem that he wanted to think out while he was walking. But as soon as that thought had occurred to her, it was sharply contradicted by a simple and unreasoning conviction that he had decided to go walking by himself, because, when it came to the point, he did not want to be present at a meeting between her and Martin.

Just then she did not wish to meet Martin either, so instead of going into the bar, from which Myra's clear, high, angry voice reached her, Helen went looking for Bertie.

He was in his office, dealing with a pile of letters on his desk. When he saw her, his square, pink face took on a hunted expression. He did not smile or show any pleasure at seeing her.

" Yes ? " he said brusquely, almost rudely.

She told him that she would like a room for the night.

" Yes, yes," he said impatiently, making it clear that he wanted to go on with his work. Then he relented. " Look, I'm sorry, Miss Gamlen," he said. " I'm in a terribly nervous state, I don't know what I'm doing. It's all these people coming here, taking rooms, asking questions. At this time of year it isn't right, it isn't normal to have so many people staying here. And the questions ! Something's going to happen, I know, something terrible. And that isn't what I came to Burnstone for. I came here for the country life and the peace and quiet, because of my nerves." He thrust wild fingers through his bristling grey hair. " Oh God, my nerves ! " he moaned. " I wish I were running a restaurant in Soho. D'you know what they're saying in Burnstone, Miss Gamlen ? "

" Something about the Collivers ? "

" Yes, indeed ! I contradict it. I say I have positive information that Mrs. Colliver's in Switzerland——"

" Why in Switzerland, Bertie? "

" Well, it's a place people do go to, isn't it ? You see, I can't bear it, I simply can't bear it when people say that husband of hers has buried her in the garden. I don't mean because I believe it. Nobody believes it, that's why they go on saying it. And they point to the way he's been digging lately, as if his life depended on it, and they say a man like him doesn't suddenly start doing that without a reason. And they know that isn't true because people do all sorts of things without any reason—

I do myself often, often—but every night here in the bar I hear them saying it and I think I'm going to be sick just from imagining it."

Helen murmured something sympathetic, then said thoughtfully, " He gardens a great deal now, does he ? "

" Every day," Bertie said. " Every day and all weathers dressed up in a duffle coat and wellington boots. I've seen him myself."

" Did you by any chance see him yesterday ? "

" Not yesterday, I didn't go out. But Tom Burkall did. He came into the bar at lunch-time and said, ' He's at it again, digging, digging.' Just like that. They don't need to say any more whom they're talking about—he's just He, as if they never thought of anyone else."

" You're sure that was yesterday."

" Oh yes."

" In a duffle coat and wellington boots," Helen said slowly. That was how Elvin Colliver had been dressed when she had seen him digging, with the hood over his head to protect him from the rain. " Well, thanks, Bertie. I'll go and get some lunch now."

He nodded gloomily, adding, as she left the office, " You understand, if they really believed it they'd go to the police, or they'd go and dig that garden up themselves to see what's in it. The trouble is, they just half-believe. That's why they won't do anything about it or forget about it, but just talk, talk."

" I know," Helen said, " that's what we're all like."

She closed the door of the office behind her and was turning towards the dining-room when Martin came suddenly out of the bar.

He stood still abruptly when he saw her.

Making an obvious effort to speak calmly, he said, " My mother told me you were down here." His face was flushed and his eyes were abnormally bright. At the same time, he looked haggard and exhausted. He did not move towards her but stood there, looking tense and on the defensive, as if he expected to be accused of something.

With a pang of fear, though why this should be Helen

did not know, she realised that Martin himself was afraid, perhaps not actually of her, though from the way that he was staring at her, even that did not seem impossible, but as least of something of which she was a part. And under the fear she sensed an anger that was near the point of becoming uncontrollable.

As she had not spoken, he went on, " I've got to speak to you. Where can we go ? " There was a roughness in his voice that was unfamiliar.

" We could go and have lunch," she said.

" Alone," he said. " I've got the car. Come on, let's get away from here."

" Only for a little while, then."

" Why does it matter for how long ? "

" Because there's someone I want to see here this afternoon."

" Dreydel ? "

" Yes."

" Martin ! " It was Myra's voice. She had just come out of the bar, followed by Hovard. " I heard what you said. You are not to go away. You are not to take the car. I want you here." She was looking extraordinarily like Martin, her eyes brilliant, her colour high. " Come and have lunch with me. Helen can come too."

" And Hovard ? " Martin said, turning on her furiously. " As always, Hovard ? "

Hovard started to say something but it was lost in an attack of sneezing. His cold seemed to have returned, for his face was as puffy and his eyes were running as badly as the evening before. The sight seemed to rouse Myra to mockery, not to compassion.

" Harold ought to be in bed with two hot-water bottles instead of breathing his germs over everybody," she said. " If he'd stop swallowing his wretched pills instead of doing the normal, sensible things, he might get better. But he's determined to be his own walking advertisement. Well, Martin, are you coming ? "

" No," he said.

" I want you to come," she said in a low voice.

" I do not want to," he answered.

She turned swiftly to Helen, who saw the apprehension in her eyes.

"Helen, don't go with him, keep him here," she begged. "He won't tell me what he's been doing, he won't admit he was at that house and I'm scared. I don't want to let him out of my sight."

"You never have, have you?" Martin said. Helen had never heard him use that tone to his mother. "That was how I lost Helen."

"Listen, listen, all of you," Hovard said thickly through his handkerchief. "If you'd seen as much trouble caused by unkind words as I have, you wouldn't be turning on your nearest and dearest in this way. You'll regret it—sooner or later one always regrets it. Now why don't we all go and have lunch together——" He had to break off at that point as another fit of sneezing shook him.

"Helen," Martin said, "are you coming?"

Helen hesitated and as she did so, Myra gripped her arm.

"Don't!" Myra cried. "Keep him here. You're the only one who can. Tell him to stay. I don't know what's the matter with him, but he's gone half-crazy."

"Why don't you stay, Martin?" Helen said.

With a curse, Martin turned on his heel and walked out of the door. They heard the car outside start and drive away.

With a perverse feeling of satisfaction, Helen said, "You see, Myra, I haven't as much power over him as you—feared or hoped, whichever it was."

Myra looked at her oddly. "I think you did that on purpose. You could have put it so that he would have stayed."

"So could you, if it comes to that," Helen said.

"Well, let's go and have lunch anyway," Myra said. "I'm starving."

Helen had lunch with Myra and Hovard. It was a relief to Helen to be spared the interview with Martin in his present mood, yet she knew that she ought not to have let him go alone. It was not that she was expecting him to disappear again immediately. She felt fairly certain that he wanted to talk to her and that he would soon return for this purpose. But she had so many things to ask him and she knew that she ought not to have missed the chance of doing so.

Besides that, she thought, in one way or another she was always letting Martin down. Because of her shrinking from some of his more explosive moods, she almost invariably failed him when he seemed most to need her.

After lunch she separated from Myra and Hovard and went up to her room. But almost immediately a maid followed her to tell her that Miss Colliver had called and wanted to see her. As she went downstairs, Helen thought that she ought almost to have expected a visit from either Mignon or her brother, to explain Mignon's screaming and fainting when she read the name of Evelyn Lander.

Wrapped in a long brown tweed cape, Mignon was in the lounge. She looked grotesquely out of place in the cheerful room. She did not speak when Helen appeared, but her prominent eyes searched Helen's anxiously.

" Are you feeling better ? " Helen asked.

She noticed that Mignon's breathing was rapid.

" I feel a little strange," Mignon answered. " I can't describe it to you, this feeling, this . . . No, I don't know a name for it. I've had a very extraordinary experience. I want to tell you about it and to ask your opinion. At the moment I'm too amazed to be able to think properly, and I can't—in a moment I'll explain that to you—I can't discuss it with Elvin, yet I must talk to somebody."

Helen nodded and sat down in a chintz-covered chair. Mignon, gathering her heavy cape closely around her, as if she found the mere cleanliness of the room and the brightness of the fire chilling, crouched in another chair.

" I'm going to be perfectly honest with you and begin by making a confession," she said. " Unless I do that I shan't be able to explain the shock I've had. I shan't be able to make you understand why I felt such—such terror and amazement, when I saw what I'd written.

Elvin says I also gave a scream. I don't remember that. In fact, I don't remember any of it very clearly from the time that the music began, and of course that's all part of it. . . . You see, my dear, that was a *genuine* message."

Helen could almost have sworn that at that moment tears came into Mignon's eyes.

" Then the others . . . ? "

" Yes, yes, that's just it," Mignon said, her low voice dropping to an even vaguer whisper than usual. " Fakery, my dear, all of them—or nearly all of them. Years ago, when I began, there were a few which I truly believe were genuine. They came quite by accident. I was fiddling with a pencil, a blue pencil, correcting some wretched essay by a child. I was a school-mistress in those days and very unhappy in the work. I've never had any understanding of children. And I went into a kind of daydream, as I often did, a deep and beautiful daydream, and when I came out of it, I found that I had written several words right across this child's work. And I hadn't had the faintest knowledge of having written anything, and the words themselves were very beautiful and very comforting to a lonely young woman, such as I was. And that wasn't the only message I had. For a little while there were others, all very beautiful and full of a deep meaning which I felt quite certain could never have come out of my own mind. I was perfectly convinced that I was in communication with some rare and wonderful individuality."

She gave a convulsive shudder.

" But my mistake, my terrible mistake was that I thought I had some control over this power to communicate with the unseen," she said. " I thought that some of the joy and comfort that had come to me through it could be given to my poor brother, who was then sorrowing deeply because a young woman whom he loved, and to whom he had believed himself to be engaged to be married, had suddenly married another. But as soon as I approached the matter with a purpose in my mind, the gift departed. Nothing came to me, nothing at all.

And so—so I started to make up little messages to cheer poor Elvin, who has had a great deal of misfortune in his life, particularly with women. They leave him or they die. So my deception, I believe, has been more than justified, though the cost to me . . . Well, I leave you to imagine it."

"At what point did your brother begin to co-operate in the frauds?" Helen asked.

"Elvin *co-operate* . . . !" It was gasped in an indignant tone. But then Mignon gave a tremulous sigh. "Not till much later and then most unwillingly. I take all the blame. I had, I confess, realised that there were certain small commercial possibilities in my gift, and I so disliked teaching. . . . But at the beginning it was all pure and sincere. And now—now when I'm so unworthy, it suddenly returns to me! Can you imagine what that means to me? Can you imagine what I felt when I saw on that paper words that I knew I had not written?"

There was so much emotion in the way that she had spoken, that Helen was almost ready to think that Mignon believed what she had said. For a moment, asking herself if it was conceivable that Dreydel's hoax had actually deceived this experienced hoaxer, Helen nearly forgot that it might be a matter of deepest importance to the Collivers to explain away Mignon's terror on reading what Dreydel had written.

"Do you know what it meant?" Helen asked.

"Ah no," Mignon said quickly, "but there's nothing strange in that. It may be that I shall have further messages—that's my profound hope—that will give me illumination. But at the moment this name Evelyn Lander is completely unknown to me. There's only one thing about it that I fear I do understand. I think, I feel almost certain, that I was being told indirectly that poor Violet is dead. And that's partly what I want to ask your opinion about."

"My only opinion about it all," Helen said, "is that if you really believe that, you should go to the police."

"Elvin's already done that," Mignon said.

"He *has*?" In spite of the fact that this was what

Elvin Colliver had said he would do, Helen had not expected it to happen.

" He's gone nearly crazy with anxiety," Mignon said. " He rushed along to the police-station as soon as you left, then because he thought Sergeant Makin was a little slow in taking in what he told him, he got on his bicycle and went straight off to London."

" On a bicycle—from here ? "

" No, only as far as Oxford on his bicycle, then he'll take the train. He said he was going to Scotland Yard and I shouldn't be surprised if he really does. Once Elvin's made up his mind about anything, no one can stop him. And he worshipped poor Violet, although his marriage to her was so disappointing."

" Through your intervention, wasn't it ? " Helen said. " Though I'd thought that he was probably in on the scheme too."

Mignon's mouth opened. She seemed to have been caught off guard and for an instant Helen saw a different person looking at her out of the prominent eyes, a shrewd, swift-thinking yet very frightened person.

" I don't know what you mean," Mignon said.

" Mr. Dreydel and I found the messages from Mr. Delborne," Helen said, " the ones that got my aunt to go away from here. And you've just told me yourself that none of them was genuine."

" I see. Yes." Mignon's eyelids drooped, as if she knew that her look had revealed too much. " You're quite right, of course—they weren't genuine. They were a trick that Elvin and I played on poor Violet to get her to go away, but I beg you to believe me that we had only her good at heart—her safety. Yes, her safety. You see, we've known for a long time that her life was in danger."

She raised her eyelids slowly. Her eyes had regained their customary look of emotional intensity.

" That's why Elvin's gone straight to Scotland Yard," she said. " We've done our best to keep her hidden. We never let anyone but you know where she was and I was against telling even you, but Elvin said that would be too unkind. But as soon as you'd seen her and been reassured that all was well with her, we made her move and we didn't mean you to find her again. I don't know how you did."

"What's she in danger from?" Helen asked.

Mignon edged forward in her chair and whispered, "That man Hovard—he's mad to get hold of the house, you know. He's been up to see us about it again and again, as if it was in our power to sell it. At first we couldn't understand it at all, either why he wanted it so much or why he kept coming to us when he knew we couldn't do anything about it. And he was ready to pay far more than it's worth. Then we discovered how he made his money and after that of course it was clear."

"He makes his money out of patent medicines," Helen said. "But that doesn't tell me why he should want to murder my aunt."

"But it does tell you why he wants the house so badly," Mignon said. "It's for the address, that's all. Hovard, Ltd., Burnstone. It would mean that he could put his wretched products on the market with almost the same name as the drugs put out by Hovard and Hayle. They're a well-known firm, aren't they, with an excellent reputation. Well, I expect he'd make his label as like theirs as he dared and deceive a lot of people. A nasty dishonest business, but there you are, that's what people are like."

"Do you know this for certain, or are you just guessing?" Helen asked.

"You can call it guessing, if you want to," Mignon said, "but it makes sense, doesn't it?"

"As to why he should want the house, yes, I should think you're probably right. But I'm afraid I don't see it as a good reason for a murder."

"Don't you—not when you're going to get a rich widow thrown in, because now that poor Violet's probably dead, that's what Mrs. Andras will be. Quite rich. And that brings me back to what I wanted to ask your advice about . . ."

"Just a moment," Helen said. "You want me to believe that Harold Hovard has been plotting for a long time to kill my aunt, in order to get hold of the house for his business purposes and to make Myra Andras worth marrying, and that you and your brother, realising this, have been trying to protect my aunt by keeping her hidden from him."

Mignon nodded her head several times. " You've such a clear mind," she murmured.

Helen wanted to say that she did not think her mind was nearly as clear as Mignon's, or as quick. Instead, she said, " Where were you yesterday, Miss Colliver ? "

Mignon started. " I ? I was at home. Why do you want to know ? "

" Just an idea I had," Helen said. " Did you see anyone ? "

" Only Elvin."

" No one else at all—all day ? "

" No—yes, I did though. I spoke to Mr. and Mrs. Hindmarch over the garden wall. I think that was yesterday, but I've so little sense of time. Why do you want to know, Helen ? You're almost frightening me."

" Never mind," Helen said. " What was it you wanted to ask my advice about ? "

But Helen's questions seemed to have disconcerted Mignon, so that she could not think what she had wanted to ask. After staring in silence at Helen, she got to her feet, and apparently lost in thought, walked slowly towards the door. Before she reached it, she paused and said, " I wanted to ask you if you thought I should go to Mrs. Andras and tell her that the house is now probably hers and that Elvin and I will of course leave it as soon as there is any evidence—concrete evidence—that Violet's dead. That's what we should both prefer to do. Alas, it hasn't been a happy home for us, in spite of its beauty. On the other hand, it seems to me that it might be our duty to wait until—well, until there's been some possibility of unmasking that man Hovard and saving Mrs. Andras from his clutches."

" For the present," Helen said, " I should wait."

" You think so ? Yes, I'm afraid you're right." Sighing as if this conclusion were a burden to her, Mignon turned back to the door.

Helen waited for a moment after she had gone, then went upstairs to her room. She opened the door, took a couple of steps forward, then stopped dead, staring in horror at what lay on her bed.

Then she began to scream.

XVI

HER SCREAMS had several results. One was that they brought Myra hurrying from her room. Another was that they brought Bertie out of his office downstairs, not quite screaming himself, but shouting wildly to know what was the matter. The third and most important result was that the sounds affected the body that lay on Helen's bed, drawing a groan from it and a faint movement, so that she realised that Martin was not dead.

By the time that she had reached his side, he had opened his eyes. He seemed uncertain where he was. Trying to sit up, he clasped his hands to his head and at once dropped back flat on the bed. Instead of groaning, he started some quiet but healthy cursing.

Helen and Myra, together, started demanding to know what had happened. But then at the same time they had the idea that the first thing was to get a doctor.

"I'll go," Helen said and ran out into the passage, where she bumped into Bertie, who also had his hands to his head and looked as if he were in as much pain and confusion as Martin.

"It's happened!" he cried. "I've been waiting for it and now it's come!"

"We want Dr. Pepall," Helen said. "Can you get him for us, Bertie?"

Bertie was still listening to imaginary screams, tearing apart the quiet of his hotel.

"I can't bear it," he said. "I can't bear loud noises and excitement. Something's got to be done about it. It's got to be stopped."

Helen thrust her face close to his.

" We want a doctor, Bertie," she said. " Dr. Pepall, if you can get him. Mr. Andras has had an accident."

" Is he alive or dead ? " Bertie asked, with a sudden return of his busy, practical manner and sounding as if he were merely anxious to get the details straight.

" Alive—but hurry, do please hurry ! "

Nodding briskly, Bertie ran down the stairs. Helen returned to her bedroom.

She found Martin, on the bed, frantically searching through his pockets. She could see no sign of any injury on him, but he was very pale. Myra, standing close to him, had her hands clasped together, while her face was almost as pale as his.

" For God's sake," she was saying, " tell me what it is and I'll find it for you. You never can find anything. Lie still—you ought to be lying still—and I'll look for it."

" It's gone," Martin muttered. " It's no good looking for it."

" But if you'd just tell me what it is——"

" He took it, it's no good looking for the damned thing ! " Yet he went on with his feverish search. " That's what he wanted, that's why he knocked me out."

" Who did ? " Helen asked.

" You're damned friend, Dreydel," Martin answered. In the pallor of his face, his eyes blazed with rage. " He came at me from behind and knocked me out and took it."

" Took *what* ! " Myra repeated.

Martin was emptying his pockets on to the bed, handling each thing that came out of them as if he thought that it might in some way be concealing the object, whatever it was, that he had lost. He was not only furious at his loss, Helen thought. He was also very frightened.

" I wish you'd lie down again and keep still," Myra said. She also looked frightened, but this was probably for the simple reason that she was still far from sure that Martin was unhurt. " The doctor's coming."

" I don't want a doctor," Martin said, " I'm perfectly all right. I want to find . . . But he took the damn' thing, it's gone. I know it's no use looking." There was almost a sob in his voice.

" How d'you know it was Mr. Dreydel ? " Helen asked. " If he came at you from behind, how can you tell who it was ? "

" All right, it was Bertie, it was Colliver, it was anyone you like," Martin said bitterly. " Only, as it happens, it was Dreydel."

" Did you actually see him ? " Helen insisted.

Without answering, Martin started to get up. But at once he swayed and clasped his head. Myra took him by the shoulders and put all her small weight into thrusting him back on to the bed.

Giving in to her and lying back with one arm thrown across his eyes, he said, " No, I didn't actually see him. But I did see him go upstairs just ahead of me and go to his room. And just before I blacked out I heard his door open and heard his step in the passage. At least . . ." He suddenly sounded less sure of himself. " I think that's how it happened."

" And what were you doing in here, anyway ? " Helen asked.

" Need you keep pestering him ? " Myra asked fiercely. " I should have thought your questions could wait until after the doctor's been."

Helen thought that they probably could and half-realised that the ruthlessness of her questioning just then was part of the reaction after the shock of finding Martin, as she had believed, dead and probably murdered on her bed. But she could not stop herself.

" What were you doing here ? " she asked again.

" Looking for you," Martin said.

" Why ? "

" Why ! " Myra said. " Because he never does anything else. And you keep pretending you don't know it, playing hell with his life and his work and his nerves——"

" Mother ! " Martin said furiously.

Myra shrugged her shoulders and went towards the door.

" I think I'll leave you two to each other's so tender mercies," she said. " I'll see if Bertie's really been trying to get Dr. Pepall."

When she had gone, there was silence. Then Martin, with his eyes still closed, held out his hand to Helen.

" Come here," he said.

She came to him, putting her hand in his and sitting down on the edge of the bed beside him.

" Don't take any notice of what she says," he said. " She's been having a bad time lately. She's in love, you know, in love with that man Hovard. I don't know why. He isn't the only man who's wanted her since my father died. He isn't the only lover she's had. But he's the only one she's wanted to marry. I don't know what he's got that's done it, but there it is. And at the same time she understands him. She knows all that there is to know about him—except that he's been in gaol. I don't think she actually knows that."

Helen felt his fingers tighten on hers. She laid her other hand on top of his, absently stroking it.

" Are you sure of all this ? " she asked quietly.

" Yes, I've had someone looking into it," he said. " He was in gaol for fraud of some sort."

" I mean, are they really going to get married ? "

" Unless I can stop it."

" How can you do that ? "

" Perhaps I can't. But there are several things I can try."

" Is that what you've been doing since I saw you last ? "

He opened his eyes, but as if the light hurt them, shut them quickly again.

" I've been looking for your aunt," he said.

" And you found her, didn't you ? "

" Yes."

" But you didn't let me know, as you said you would."

" I was going to."

" Where is she now, Martin ? "

He started, opening his eyes again.

" I don't know," he said. " You've been out to Barnet

yourself, my mother told me. You've seen all that I saw."

"You mean she wasn't there when you were there?"

"No."

"What time was that?"

"I don't know. Sometime in the afternoon. I rang several times but didn't get any answer."

"Yet you went in and came out again with a big trunk, which you put in your car." Drawing her hand away from him, she stood up. "Don't bother to think up a lie. You were seen."

He gave a bitter smile. "Not by you, was it?"

"No."

"But you've decided to believe whoever it was who said they'd seen me, rather than wait to hear what I've got to say."

"Well, wasn't it you with the trunk?"

"No." As he said it, his hand strayed to the little heap of objects that had come out of his pockets. Picking them up one by one, he started putting them back where they had come from. "I suppose it was your friend Dreydel who said he'd seen me—the pleasant character who jumps on people from behind and picks their pockets."

"No, it was the woman next door."

"She doesn't know me."

Helen sat down again on the edge of the bed and caught hold of both his hands. "Martin, it *was* you, I know it was you. I don't know what you were doing with the trunk, but I'm certain it was you. And I've got a feeling that if I'd gone with you before lunch, you'd have told me about it."

"But you didn't go with me." His gaze had become hard and unfriendly. "And when I came looking for you, I got knocked on the head by your friend."

"You don't really know who did that."

"It was Dreydel."

"Martin, please——" She had a feeling that it was a matter of terrible urgency to make him tell her the truth about the trunk. "What was in the trunk? Where did you take it?"

" There wasn't any trunk." But his voice altered as he said this, faltering slightly, while his gaze, meeting hers, lost the bright glitter of antagonism and suspicion. " Helen, I haven't done anything awful—don't believe that of me—don't. I had to do what I did. There wasn't any other way I could think of. I had to do something to save my mother from ruining her whole life. That man's bad, Helen. You probably think that's just jealousy on my part, the old story about the son and the mother—but that isn't it at all. I tell you, I can feel it about him, that he's something really vile. You think so too, don't you ? You can feel it ? "

" I can understand your not wanting her to marry a man who's been in gaol——"

" It isn't just that. It's a feeling I get about him every time I see them together. And he knows I get that feeling, because he's been working on her to get me out of the way. He's afraid that I'll be able to prove something bad enough against him to upset this infatuation of hers. And I will—give me a little time and I will. Time— just a little. That's what I need. That's why I had to——"

There was a knock on the door.

It was the doctor. Helen had been waiting for him impatiently, because Martin's pallor, together with his growing excitement, had renewed her anxiety, yet she wished that something could have delayed the inter- ruption for a few minutes. Martin had reached the point, she believed, where he wanted to confide in her; and in another moment would have told her the truth about the trunk. Whether or not he would be in the same state of mind when Dr. Pepall left was a matter of doubt.

Leaving them together, she went downstairs, finding Myra and Harold Hovard in the lounge. Myra called out to her.

" Come here, Helen. I've been talking over this extraordinary event with Harold and we both want to know what you think. Was it Mr. Dreydel who attacked Martin ? "

It was the last thing that Helen wanted to discuss with

them, or with anyone just then. She wanted to find Dreydel, or, if she could not find him, to have a little time to herself to discover what she believed about the assault on Martin.

If Dreydel had done it, then she wanted never to see him again. So much was simple. But was it conceivable that he had done it? What possible reason could he have had for it? Unless he had been deceiving her from start to finish about the reason for his interest in the Collivers, what could he want from Martin so badly that he would knock him on the head to get it?

Myra was insisting, "You brought Mr. Dreydel into this, Helen. What do you know about him?"

"Not much," Helen said.

"But you did bring him into the affair."

"I didn't. He has reasons of his own for taking an interest in Shipley's End."

"Shipley's End?" Hovard said sharply. "You don't mean he's after it too? But it doesn't matter, Shipley's End is not for sale." He smiled at Myra and laid a hand possessively over one of hers.

To Helen's surprise, Myra snatched it away.

"We'll see," she said. "Perhaps it is for sale. Who knows what I should decide to do with it if—if it were mine. Does your friend Dreydel want to buy it, Helen?"

"Not to my knowledge," Helen said.

"Then why's he interested in it? And what was the reason for that show he put on at the Collivers, pretending he believed in Mignon's powers. And who's Evelyn Lander?"

"You'd better ask him when he comes in," Helen answered. "I really know very little about him."

"Where is he?"

"He went out for a walk."

"But Martin said——"

"Martin doesn't really know what happened to him," Helen said.

Harold Hovard interrupted them at this point by a violent attack of sneezing. Myra looked at him with contempt.

" Poor man," she said ironically. " Isn't he a sight, Helen ? And he'll still tell you that he hasn't really got a cold and that his wretched pills will cure him. Pathetic, isn't it ? "

Hovard blew his nose and mopped his eyes and managed to smile at Helen.

" The little lady likes to pretend that she's got a very hard heart, but I know better," he said.

" Do you ? " Myra said. Helen was astonished at the anger in her tone. " Do you really think so ? Because you could be quite wrong, my dear. You could easily discover that my heart was as hard as stone."

He shook his head, still smiling.

" She's worried about the boy," he said. " She's the kind who starts hitting out at everything near them whenever they're badly worried about something."

In that, Helen thought, he was probably speaking the truth. Myra would always find it difficult to admit simply to a serious worry, because that would feel almost like admitting to a defeat. It would mean betraying the fact that she did not feel herself, just then, to be mistress of her fate and that events had power over her.

" Well, I don't mind," Hovard went on, turning his smile on her. " If it helps you, slam away."

" Don't tempt me," she answered softly, then she got up and walked towards the stairs to meet Dr. Pepall, who was coming down them.

He was followed by Martin, who was still pale but looked less shaky than before. Reassuring Myra briefly, Dr. Pepall hurried to the door. His eyes, as he went, encountered Helen's and flashed her a signal of some sort. Following him out, she found that he had not paused to wait for her but was already getting into his car. However, when he saw her, he said, " Good, I wanted a word with you, Helen. That young man, there's nothing the matter with him, but he's had a shock of some sort. Keep an eye on him, if you can."

" A shock ? " she said.

" I don't mean the bump on the head. He told me, by the way, he'd slipped and hit his head against the bedpost. We'll let it go at that, shall we? But the shock I mean is something emotional, and I don't like the look of it. I'd say offhand that he is in the grip of some unholy terror. Know anything about that?"

She hesitated. "I'm not sure. Dr. Pepall——"

"Yes?"

"May I ask you about something quite different? It's about my aunt."

"Oh yes, I meant to ask you, how is she?" he said.

"That's what I wanted to ask you," Helen said. "Was she—is she—seriously ill?"

He hesitated now, then he nodded.

"I'm afraid so, Helen. It's her heart."

"So ill she might die at any moment?"

"Yes. Though if she was lucky and took great care of herself . . ."

"Why didn't you tell me before?" she asked.

"She wouldn't let me." He was watching her carefully. "Has something happened?"

"I think so, but—I know it sounds strange—I don't really know. I don't know *what's* happened."

"Can I help in any way?"

"I don't think so."

"If I can, let me know," he said as he started his car.

Helen, turning back to the doorway of the Swan, met Martin coming hurriedly out of it.

At first she thought that he was looking for her, but when he saw her he took no notice of her, but turned on Myra, who had followed him out.

"Where've you put the car?" he demanded.

It was only then that Helen realised that the Andras's car, which had been parked near the door, was not there now.

Myra looked vaguely up and down the street.

"I didn't move it," she said.

"Did Hovard?"

"Perhaps. No, I don't think so. Where would he get the keys?"

"Yes, where would he—where would anyone?"

Martin had started another frantic search through his

pockets, spilling loose change, cigarettes and pencil-stubs on to the steps of the Swan and muttering, " I wasn't thinking of them before. I didn't look for them. I haven't got them." He spun on his heel and strode back into the building.

Myra went hurrying after him, reminding him that the car was insured, that he was anyway not in a fit state to drive it and begging him with a degree of emotion that sounded strange in her clear, light voice, not to get too excited. Helen stayed behind to collect the objects that Martin had sprayed over the steps.

As she did so, she heard Bertie's excited voice in the lobby.

" Yes, I saw it, I tell you—I saw it just before Miss Gamlen started screaming—and then I forgot about it because of the screams. But I saw it."

" You saw Dreydel drive off in my car ? " Martin said.

" Yes," Bertie said, " there couldn't be any doubt about it."

XVII

HELEN LET the pennies and sixpences, the cigarettes and the pencil-stubs slide out of her fingers back on to the steps. Straightening up, she realised that she was shivering. The afternoon, all of a sudden, felt terribly cold.

Her hands began to fumble with the buttons of her coat. She fastened it up to her neck, then thrust her hands into her pockets and walked off quickly down the street.

She remembered, as she went, how the blackened leaves in the ditches had reminded her that morning of death and of winter. Immediately after that she found herself wondering if she would ever come to Burnstone again. Never, she thought, if she could help it. Shipley's End would always be haunted by the whispering of Mignon's false ghosts, while the bright, welcoming rooms of the Swan would be haunted by other falsities and lies that in truth would hurt even longer and more deeply.

But why had he done it? Why had Nicholas Dreydel assaulted Martin, picked his pockets and stolen his car? And why had he told her his fearful stories of murdered women, making her believe him, making her accept his explanation of what had happened in that house in Barnet, filling her mind so full with the thought of murder that she had scarcely looked for other explanations? What had he really wanted all the time?

She remembered how much she had distrusted him at first, and how at times since then the distrust had returned but had always faded again because of something in him that had seemed truthful, direct and strong. After this, she thought, she would never be able to trust her own feelings again.

The sun was low in the sky already, shining into her eyes. She walked towards it without thinking of where she was going. Somebody in passing her said good-evening and she answered mechanically. Rage was growing in her, a cold rage that made her unable to think about anything but the rage itself, while her body responded to it by this blind, swift walking ahead.

Knowing as she now did that Dreydel had stolen Martin's car and the keys from his pocket, she no longer had any doubt left that it was Dreydel who had attacked Martin and the thought of this, all the more because at first she had refused to believe it of him, was unbearable. In her walking she was trying both to escape from the facts and to work some sort of violence upon them.

It was the sinking of the sun, in the last moments so disconcertingly sudden, and the immediate change around her from a gold-streaked daylight to chill shadow, that at last made her pause, remembering uneasily two things. One was that Dr. Pepall had asked her to keep an eye on Martin. The other was that for some reason, for some time, she had trusted Nicholas Dreydel.

Walking more slowly, then standing still, seeing in the sky the last traces of a dim, bronze, wintry sunset shining through leafless branches, the feeling of trust, not as an active emotion but as a bewildering memory, came back to her. Detached from it, considering it in herself as something almost alien, she turned and began walking back to the Swan.

Her face wore a puzzled frown. Yet something in her mind was becoming clearer. By the time that she had reached the Swan, she had discovered what she intended to do next, though there had been no reasoning in the decision. It was simply that there seemed to be nothing else that she could do. Not the circumstances but her own nature blotted out the possibility of any alternative.

On her way in she again gathered up from the steps the contents of Martin's pockets which no one else had yet thought of collecting, then she went looking for him. She found him alone in the lounge. When she came in he was standing with his back to her, close to the fire, looking down at it intently, while both his hands gripped the edge of the mantelshelf. She could see how hard they were gripping it, as if he would have liked to break it.

When she spoke to him, he started violently, then gave her an unexpected smile, which was uncertain and diffident, but came at the same time as a look of deep relief in his eyes.

" I couldn't think where you'd gone," he said.

She held out his belongings. " You dropped these around," she said. " You shouldn't be so careless."

" No, I shouldn't, should I ? Thanks." His voice was subdued. " I am careless. That thing I thought I'd lost—and the car-keys—I dare say I just left them around somewhere."

" No," Helen said, " I know he took them."

" We don't know that for sure. I didn't really see him, you know. You were quite right about that. It could have been anyone."

" But he took your car."

" Bertie may have been mistaken."

" No," she said, " you know he wasn't."

" Well, don't look so tragic about it. He probably had his reasons."

She looked at him in astonishment. Putting an arm round her, Martin drew her close to him.

"It's all right," he said, "I know you're in love with him. And there's no need for you to worry about him. He'll be back."

She leant away from him, looking into his face, then lowered hers, resting it against him.

"I was going to tell you about it," she said. "I meant to tell you about it, and then ask you . . . ."

"What?"

"What really happened up there?"

"And I'd made up my mind I was going to tell you."

His hand was on her hair, singularly gentle. She stayed quite still, wondering at this mood in him.

"I came down here to find you, you know," he said. "I knew I'd got to tell you what I'd done. And then—then I saw my mother first, and she messed it all up. That's what she's always done, hasn't she? Only it wasn't really her fault, it was mine as much as hers. It was she you used really to be jealous of, wasn't it?"

"I suppose it was," Helen said. "I think you've always loved her far more than anyone else."

"I don't know. Perhaps. It didn't always feel like love. And during these last weeks it's been . . . I can't describe it."

"But you came to me that evening because of her, didn't you?"

"Yes."

"Because of her and Hovard."

"Yes, I wanted to tell you all about it. But you were so . . ."

"I know, I didn't help much."

With some of his usual vehemence, he said, "You seemed to hate me! I couldn't talk to you, I couldn't say a thing. So I just asked you about your aunt and tried to worry you as much as I could, partly, I suppose, because I wanted a sort of revenge on you for letting me down, because that was how it felt. In spite of the way that everything between us had gone wrong, I'd always

161

had a feeling that you were there—that at least some part of you was there for me, though I didn't think about that until after I'd seen you and realised that there wasn't anything there for me at all."

"That isn't true," she said, "I was awfully afraid of finding that there was as much as ever. If I'd understood what you really wanted . . ."

"Well, you know that part of it now. I wanted to find out if your aunt was alive. There were those stories around in Burnstone that she was dead. I didn't really believe them, but I knew what it would mean if they were true. Hovard would marry my mother. But I didn't think he'd marry her without the house and the money. So I wanted you to find your aunt for me. But then, when you did, it turned out that she was behaving in such an extraordinary way that I got suspicious—I didn't know of what—but I even wondered if Hovard was at the back of it somehow."

"That's what Mignon Colliver tried to make me think," Helen said.

But Martin was in that state now where he seemed not to hear anything that was said to him, but could only follow his own thoughts.

"Then you brought Dreydel in and I thought he was a detective," he said. "So then I decided to take a hand in things too and I came down here to watch Colliver, thinking he'd lead me to your aunt sooner or later. And he did and I went to see her and I asked her——"

"She was alive ! " Helen said with a gasp.

"Of course, she . . ." He stopped. "This was a week ago, not yesterday."

"But yesterday—you saw her yesterday ! "

"I'll come to that in a moment." His voice had suddenly gone hoarse. "I want to tell this in my own way. I went to see her and I asked her to tell me why she was ducking from pillar to post. I asked her if she was afraid of anyone and if I could help her. She started crying and said she was so tired and felt so ill, and then she said she was terribly afraid, only not of anything human, and than she started talking a great deal about my uncle, and it almost sounded as if she were afraid of him."

" Whyever didn't you tell me you'd found her ? " Helen exclaimed.

" Because she told me not to."

" But still, if she was in that state . . ."

" She begged me not to, saying that if I did, she'd move again. I think she said she'd *have* to move again, still as if that were somehow to do with my uncle. And she said she was so pleased with that little house, feeling almost as if it were her own. So I promised."

" Yet you told Myra."

" Yes. You see, I wanted her to know that I'd seen Mrs. Colliver and that there wasn't any doubt about her being alive. She didn't altogether trust you about that— or pretended she didn't."

" But yesterday ! " Helen repeated. " What happened yesterday, Martin ? And what did Nicholas steal from your pocket ? "

She felt a nervous tremor in his body. He looked round, as if he had only just become aware that they were in a room which other people might enter at any moment.

" Look, we can't talk about that here," he said. " Where else can we go ? "

" But you've got to tell me about that."

" Yes, but not here. Let's go out, then we can be sure no one can overhear us."

" It's getting awfully cold."

" Never mind, we can walk." He made for the door.

As they went out, she caught at his arm, half-afraid that he had said all that he meant to say and now meant to escape from her. But except that he started walking too fast for her through the twilight village, so that after a moment she had to tell him that the pace was beyond her, he showed no signs of trying to get away. Yet at first he would not or could not say any more.

He had not taken the road that led towards Shipley's End, but had gone in the opposite direction. Here the houses of the village were soon left behind them. A long row of pines cut off the view of the still faintly lighted sky and the pale glitter of the early stars, casting a deep shadow over the road. As if this darkness made him feel safe to go on talking, Martin began again as soon as they reached it.

"You're going to say now I'm mad," he said. "I probably am. Anyway, I was yesterday. Nothing in the world could ever make me do again what I did then. But at least I've come to my senses now and I can guess what I'll have to pay for it."

He said this half-questioningly, as if he hoped for some reassurance from Helen that the payment need not necessarily be as heavy as he expected. When she did not answer, he went on in a low but defiant tone, "The chances are I'm going to be arrested for murder."

Helen had been waiting for that word to be spoken, but she had not been expecting it at that moment. "So—so it *was* my aunt's body in that trunk."

"Of course," he said angrily. "You've known that all along."

"I haven't. Oh God, Martin——"

"Don't say it," he said, "don't say anything. Wait till I've told you the whole story."

"And the thing that Nicholas took from you . . ."

"Of course, of course, the receipt for the trunk. It's at King's Cross. . . . No, wait!" For she had started to speak again. "Listen to the rest of it, then say all you want to. I went out to that house yesterday to see how she was. I'd been worrying about her more and more all the week. I wanted to tell you about her. So I went out and when I didn't get any answer I nearly came away again and then something made me wander round to the back of the house. I think I'd a vague idea she might be pottering around in the garden and so might not have heard me when I rang. She wasn't, of course, but I found the back door standing open. I went in and . . . I found her."

"Dead?"

"Yes. She was slumped in a chair by the fire, with all her usual belongings around her, her work-basket

164

and her writing-case—d'you remember how we gave her that writing-case together? There were all the things there that had seemed to be a part of her for as long as I can remember her. And at first I thought she'd just died there quietly by herself. And then—then I began to notice things."

They had reached the end of the patch of shadow and passed out into the starlight. Ahead of them the road was empty, a grey streak winding away between the hedges. Martin was peering along it so intently that he might have been expecting something of great importance to him to appear there at any moment.

"There'd been a struggle," he said. "Not much of one, because she'd have been very easily overcome. But she'd been struck on the head two or three times—there was a little blood—and then I think she'd been smothered. There were some small feathers sticking to her face and on the floor there was a cushion with a small tear in the covering. And then I realised that she'd had a visitor. There were some drinks on a tray, a bottle of sherry and some gin and two glasses and one of the glasses was still half-full of gin. . . . It was when I saw that that I lost my head, Helen. Until then I swear I'd only been thinking of calling the police as fast as I could, but when I saw that I suddenly understood what had happened and I could only think of how to save my mother."

"Only it wasn't gin, Martin," Helen said. "It was water."

He seemed not to hear her. Walking onwards with his set stare on the road ahead, he seemed to be about to pour out the rest of his story. Then abruptly he stood still and for the first time since they had come out, looked into her face.

"It was water?" he said incredulously.

"Yes."

"But then . . ."

"Go on," she said. "Go on with what you did next."

"But if it was water. . . . No. it doesn't necessarily change anything—though it's Colliver, isn't it, who doesn't touch alcohol? Only I don't suppose he usually drinks water out of a cocktail glass. Could he have been humouring her, d'you think? Pretending? Because she liked to offer people drinks and . . . But Colliver's got an alibi, hasn't he? Mother said he has."

"I'm not absolutely certain about that," Helen said slowly. "I'll tell you about that presently. Go on now about what you did."

Martin brought cigarettes out of his pocket. In the flare of the match that he struck, she saw that his eyes had lost their intentness and that he seemed to be confused and fumbling for the thread of his thoughts.

"Yes, what I did . . ." He stayed still, starting to shiver in the cold. "You see, I thought Hovard had been there. I thought Mother had told him where your aunt was and that he'd gone out there and murdered her. I thought—I even thought perhaps Mother knew about it. I know now that isn't so, but for a little while I was insane, I could believe anything. And I could only think of somehow hiding your aunt's body, so that nothing could be proved against my mother, and besides—well, she—your aunt—had been acting so strangely, disappearing again and again, that I thought if she simply disappeared once more, no one would believe that she was dead and so the Collivers would keep the house and the money and Hovard would never marry my mother. So I brought that big trunk down from one of the rooms upstairs and I put the body into it and then I took it to King's Cross and left it in the cloakroom till I could think what to do with it next. And then I came looking for you. But Dreydel got the receipt from me and he's gone to the police with it, and meanwhile I've come to my senses and——" His voice cracked. "Well, there's nothing for me to do but wait."

For a long time Helen could think of nothing to say. She was shivering too, yet she could not have moved from the spot.

At last she said, "And this is all true, Martin? It's not your—well, your imagination at work, trying to cover up something for somebody else."

"It's all true."

"What a mess you've made of things," she groaned. "You know, you left one of her slippers behind and her handbag—and the cat, Martin!"

"I didn't see a cat."

"A little black kitten. Someone had locked it up in the coal-shed."

"Why should anyone do that?"

"I don't know. I suppose the murderer did it, though why he should have wasted time doing it, I don't know. With a dog it might have been different, but what harm could a kitten do?"

"It probably isn't important. An accident. Unless . . ." He was suddenly intent again, his thoughts moving on swiftly. "Suppose it scratched him, Helen. Suppose it marked him. . . . No, that won't do. If it had, he'd have killed it and taken it away with him and dropped it in a gutter somewhere—though I suppose there'd still be cat-hairs in the house to prove that there's been a cat there, so that if he had scratches on his wrists, it'd be dangerous evidence that he'd been to the house. . . . No, I don't understand it."

"It's just possible," Helen said slowly, "that Elvin Colliver couldn't bear to kill a cat—a woman, yes, but a cat, no. I can imagine that. But I still don't understand why he should need to."

"I don't understand why he should need to kill his wife," Martin said. "His interest was in keeping her alive."

"Not necessarily," Helen said. "He had a motive and he'd laid long and careful plans to kill her. It's just that alibi, and I think . . . Listen, Martin, I'm going to tell you all about it."

She spoke rapidly, telling him all that had happened to her and Dreydel the afternoon before at the house in Barnet, ending with Dreydel's theory of Colliver's motive for murdering his wife and Dr. Pepall's confirmation that Mrs. Colliver in truth was dangerously ill.

While she was speaking they started to walk slowly back towards the village. There was something almost fierce in the eagerness with which Martin listened. There was no doubt now of his taking in everything that was said to him. Whenever she paused, he prompted her with impatient questions. Several times he muttered agreement.

At last, when she stopped, he said, " So they were right here in Burnstone after all, just by instinct. He was wise, wasn't he, to try to finish the story in a London suburb? You can't get away with anything in a place like this, unless people want you to. But the alibi, Helen. How do you get round that ? "

" I'm not sure if I can get round it," she said, " but I've thought of a possibility. You know what he says he was doing all yesterday ? He says he was digging in the garden, where lots of people passing must have seen him. Well, d'you know what he wears when he gardens ? He wears a duffle-coat and gum-boots and at least when I saw him, he had the hood of the duffle-coat up over his head. And that's how people here have got used to seeing him, and if they saw a figure in a duffle-coat and gum-boots digging in the garden yesterday, they'd all take for granted that it was Elvin Colliver. But suppose it was really Mignon, in the coat with the hood up and the gum-boots and a pair of her brother's trousers. Could they have told the difference ? "

Martin gripped her elbow. He started to stride ahead as fast as when they had started out from the Swan, but this time when she tried to drag, he swept her on. She could feel his fever of excitement.

" We're going to Shipley's End," he said. " We're going to talk to Mignon before Elvin gets back—and before the police come looking for me."

After that he would say nothing more, and Helen, needing all her breath to keep up with him, asked no more questions.

Neither of them spoke again until they came in sight of the house and the garden. Then both stood still in astonishment and Martin exclaimed, " Good God, what's happening ? "

The garden was full of moving lights. Besides that,

the headlights of a car, drawn up in the drive, slanted across the garden, and in its beam a number of figures could be seen, some moving about, but most of them quietly, steadily digging.

XVIII

MR. AND MRS. HINDMARCH were in charge of operations. Seeing Helen and Martin at the gate, they came to meet them. The two short, sturdy, white-haired figures were enveloped in ancient raincoats, with sheepskin gloves on their hands. Mrs. Hindmarch had a scarf knotted over her hair, Mr. Hindmarch wore an old tweed cap. Both of them carried large torches. But these were not necessary to reveal the fact that both gentle old faces were ablaze with excitement.

" You've come," Mr. Hindmarch said. " I'm glad . . ."

" Immensely glad," Mrs. Hindmarch said.

" Because if it hadn't been that we both felt——"

"—after the most searching discussion with one another——"

"—following on our discovery this afternoon, that there really wasn't a moment to be lost——"

"—though of course if we'd realised that you were in Burnstone, we should have consulted you first——"

"—we should have written you a letter and——"

Both voices came together to round off the statement, "—obtained your formal agreement to what we are doing."

Helen and Martin looked at one another, then at the garden, which to Helen seemed to be filled with hobgoblins.

" But what have the Collivers to say to this ? " she asked.

" They've gone," both Hindmarches answered.

" Gone ? " Helen and Martin said together. Then, in embarrassment at apparently copying the conversational method of the Hindmarches, each waited unnecessarily long for the other to speak next.

" Miss Colliver too ? " Martin asked.

" Yes, first Mr. Colliver went on his bicycle, about lunch-time and Miss Colliver about an hour ago, in a taxi," Mr. Hindmarch said.

" With some luggage," Mrs. Hindmarch said.

" And without coming, as she sometimes has——"

"—to leave the key with us and ask us to take care of the cats——"

"—which we always gladly did, though I'm glad to say that she always took her tame snake with her, feeling, no doubt——"

"—that we might not altogether understand its requirements."

Martin said, " And you're digging to find Mrs. Colliver's body ! Well, I'm afraid you won't——"

Helen stopped him with a hand on his arm. " Let them dig," she said in a low voice.

Neither of the Hindmarches paid much attention to this. They started again, Mrs. Hindmarch coming first this time.

" When she left like that," she said, " she was in a state of great agitation, which I happened to notice because I was out in the garden at the time, cutting down some of the dead stuff in the herbaceous border, and I thought at once of the cats, wondering if she'd made any arrangements about them——"

"—because, little as we've cared for the Collivers," her husband went on, " we should neither of us allow dumb animals to suffer, so we went over together and found——"

"—but we should prefer you to see for yourselve what we found, since it was that that decided us that *ine time had come to put a stop to or to prove the truth of——"

The voices came together again, " —these terrible rumours that have been around in the village."

Martin put a hand on the gate and pushed it open and he and Helen walked slowly towards the house.

In the garden around them they could see many people they knew, men who had been living in Burnstone when they had come there as children, farm-labourers, shop-keepers, men who worked for Hovard and Hayle. They had divided up the garden methodically between them, and each was working in his own patch with that steady and practised swing of the spade that appears so slow and yet is in fact so swift and skilful.

"But what have the police got to say to this?" Helen asked. "Aren't you all going to get into a lot of trouble?"

Both Hindmarches answered something about their duty.

Mr. Hindmarch went on, "Sergeant Makin is wisely capable of turning a blind eye, particularly when other people are doing his work for him."

"And these rumours in the village," his wife said, "have been creating an increasingly unwholesome atmosphere. The vicar himself has been saying so and slipping remarks into his sermons about slanderous tongues."

"But I do admit," Mr. Hindmarch said, "that it required some courage to take the initiative."

"Though in the state this garden's been allowed to get into, a good digging is just what it needs," Mrs. Hindmarch ended practically. "Now look—what would you have made of that?"

They had reached the house and Mrs. Hindmarch, halting, was pointing to a card that had been pinned to the door. She flashed her torch on to it, so that Helen and Martin could read what was written there.

Scrawled in blue pencil, in a writing that Helen recognised, were the words, "To Whom It May Concern —Please look after the cats and if possible find them good homes."

"That sounds," she said, "as if she weren't coming back."

"Exactly, exactly," the Hindmarches said. "That was how it struck us immediately."

Helen turned the handle of the door and led the way in.

In the darkness inside, several pairs of small green lights flickered at them near the floor. Pressing the light-switch, she saw the cats. They looked warily at the intruders and one, the big tortoise-shell, tried to shoot past them and out into the night. Martin caught him and thrusting him back, came inside and closed the door. A small black shape, detaching itself from a larger grey one, came sidling inquisitively towards them. It looked to Helen like the kitten that she and Dreydel had found in the house in Barnet.

" Now come into the kitchen," Mrs. Hindmarch said, " and we'll show you the rest of it."

They went along the passage and into the great, stone-flagged kitchen.

If Helen had not been able to surmise quite easily what any kitchen for which Mignon Colliver had been responsible would look like, the scene in this kitchen, which she remembered as a place of tables scrubbed white, of shining pots and pans and of fine crockery on polished dresser shelves, would have been a shock. As it was, she scarcely thought about the stained boards and the grease-coated sink, the dirty rags, used for unthinkable purposes, that littered odd ledges, the food that lay about uncovered, the tea-cloths, hanging on a line and so long unwashed that in passing near them she could smell their curious sour odour. It was Martin who blenched when he saw these things. Helen, however, went straight to what the Hindmarches were excitedly pointing at.

This was row upon row of saucers on the floor, all filled with food. There was milk and fish and meat. There were the obvious left-overs of Colliver meals and dollops of cat-food that had come out of tins. The tins themselves lay on the floor under the sink.

" It looks like a sort of mad tea-party set out for the cats," Helen said, " meant to last them for several days."

" Exactly," the Hindmarches agreed.

Mrs. Hindmarch went on, " And that, together with the notice on the door, made us feel sure that the Collivers had, well . . ."

" Done a bunk," her husband said, " gone south, taken a powder."

Mrs. Hindmarch turned to look at him in amazement, and then as if she could not conceive in what corner of his mind expressions such as these could have been secretly stored away, unshared with her, murmured, " Well, I never ! "

For once her husband neither echoed nor capped it.

Helen and Martin agreed that there was a good deal of evidence that the Collivers, driven by fear or bad consciences, had vacated Shipley's End for good. The Hindmarches then left them, to continue overseeing the digging operations in the garden.

Left to themselves, Helen and Martin wandered through the house, seeing clear signs of a hurried departure. Yet the house did not seem in any way free of the presence of the Collivers. Even if they never came back, it would take great efforts to remove the traces of their occupation. But these, it seemed to Helen, went beyond the mere uncleanliness and litter. Somehow the house itself, she felt, had been affected by their presence. What was revealed that night to the two people going slowly from room to room was not that aspect of its age which meant strength and stability, but one that hinted at all the sinister cruelties and betrayals, small, intimate and unhistoric but deadly, that its old walls must have sheltered through the centuries.

" I think Mignon's left some of her ghosts behind," Helen said.

" Yes, it's haunted now," Martin said. " But that——" He paused at a window and pointed down into the garden. " That's the reason. It's the trying to keep out of one's mind what that really means. Then the meaning of it comes inside and follows one around. . . . Helen, do you really believe they're going to find something ? "

" Don't you ? " she asked.

" I suppose it all fits." Folding his arms on the window-sill, he gazed downwards with his face close to the glass. " A smallish, pasty-faced, dark-haired man—wasn't that how the girl described him, the girl they're—looking for out there ? That's Colliver all right, though the description would fit several million other men if it weren't associated with this house." He cleared his throat nervously. " Helen . . ."

" Yes."

" You haven't said anything about what I did at that house in Barnet. You haven't told me what you feel."

" I can't. I don't know. Let's not talk about it now," she said.

" Was I insane when I did it ? "

" Perhaps. We'll talk about it later."

" But I've got to know——"

" Please ! " Her voice rose sharply and uncontrollably.

Martin went tense, giving her a quick look, then turning his head away again to watch the stooping figures in the garden.

Helen had no idea how long they stayed at that window, Presently they left it, but only to stand, after a few minutes, at another. Martin soon grew restless, but Helen did not feel able to tear herself away. Yet if she wanted to wait until the gruesome operation in the garden was concluded, she supposed, she might have to wait all night.

Finding an electric fire in one of the rooms, she switched it on. But even when she stood close to it, it seemed to have no effect on the chill of the house, or the chill that was in herself.

It was about eight o'clock when Nicholas Dreydel appeared.

Helen wondered if he had been long in the garden with the diggers, or if, on arriving at the house, he had come at once to find her. He did not tell her, but she could see that he needed no explanation of what was happening. He and Martin looked sombrely, yet with curiously little interest at one another. But it was to Martin that Dreydel spoke first, stooping over the electric fire as he did so, rubbing his cold hands together.

" I've brought your car back," he remarked, almost casually.

Martin said nothing.

Dreydel went on, " I'm sorry I did what I did, but it seemed best."

" It probably was," Martin answered. There was a

dullness in his tone, as if he were completely worn out. " I suppose you've been to the police."

" No," Dreydel said, " though they're there now—at Highfield Gardens. I don't know who sent for them." He straightened up and thrust a hand into a pocket, bringing out cigarettes. " They'll find Mrs. Colliver there." He held the packet out to Martin.

Martin started. Then he reached out a hand that trembled to take a cigarette.

" Thanks," he muttered. He tried to say something more but could not until he had drawn several times at the cigarette. Then he said, " It won't help, though, will it ? I mean, it won't help me. They'll be able to tell what I did."

" I'm afraid so." Dreydel turned to Helen. " You know what that was, do you ? "

" Yes," she said, " Martin's told me everything."

Dreydel spoke to Martin again. " I suppose I know why you did it, though of all the purely lunatic actions. . . . There are penalties for that sort of thing, I imagine, though I don't know what they are. But with luck now you won't be suspected of the actual murder."

" May I ask why you didn't go to the police ? " Martin asked.

" I had an idea that Miss Gamlen would be against that course of action," Dreydel answered. He said it without emotion and without looking at her. " I went to King's Cross, recovered the trunk, took it back to Barnet and put it in the sitting-room. It was fairly dark when I got there and I don't think I was seen, and there's just a chance that the evidence of the woman next door, who said she saw you put the trunk in the car, won't be believed. In that case, you'd be safe. But I shouldn't count on that. There'll be the evidence of the cloakroom people at King's Cross, and for all you know, other people saw you. If I were you, I'd go the police, tell them the whole story and give them all the help you can."

" How can I help ? " Martin asked. He gestured at the window. " There are more than enough voluntary helpers on the job already."

It seemed to Helen that Dreydel was strangely un-interested in what was going forward in the garden.

" You can tell them what you saw in the house," he said. " You may have information they need."

" Nicholas——" Helen started to speak because she wanted to thank him, but the thankfulness that she actually felt seemed suddenly far too much to be put into words. " Is Elvin Colliver there in the house now with the police ? " she asked.

" No," Dreydel said. " I stayed and watched the house for a while from that bench, where I waited the other night. I saw Colliver go in and come running out again as if all hell was after him. He went straight to the public telephone and made a call, then got away as fast as he could. I walked away myself then, but I saw the police-car stop at the house before I was out of sight."

" I think Colliver himself sent for them," Helen said. " Mignon told me that was why he'd gone to London."

" If he did, it was before he went to the house," Dreydel said. " They were there too quickly after he'd made the call. Besides, I think it was a trunk-call."

" To Mignon," Martin said. " That's why she packed up and cleared out."

" Taking time, all the same, to provide for the cats," Helen said. " Have you seen that, Nicholas ? "

He shook his head.

" Come and look," she said.

They went to the kitchen. Some of the cats were crouched over the saucers of food, but others at once came miaowing about their ankles, making a restless complaint, perhaps at the absence of Mignon. The black kitten was there and, being smartly driven back from an attack on Helen's stockings, started a game with Dreydel's shoelaces.

He looked at the scene without expression. He seemed as little interested in the cats as in the garden.

If Martin had not been there, Helen would have asked him why this was, but it felt extraordinarily difficult to talk to him in Martin's presence. Then suddenly she thought that she knew the reason for the lack of excitement, the lifelessness, almost, of his manner.

" You're afraid you've been wrong ! " she exclaimed. " After all that's happened, you've started to wonder how it could be the Collivers—because of that alibi."

He was looking down at the kitten at his feet.

" I could have been wrong," he said slowly.

" But that alibi doesn't mean anything," she said. " Not as it stands."

" Why not ? "

" Because when Colliver gardens, he wears a duffle-coat with the hood up and wellington boots. And that would have been a perfect disguise for anyone—say, for Mignon. So unless he can prove that he spoke to somebody that day, or that somebody saw him, face to face . . ." She stopped because he did not seem to be listening.

He had just stopped and had picked up the kitten and was rubbing it softly behind the ears.

" Anyway," he said, in a way that sounded as if he were merely concluding something that he had been saying to her, " this little fellow can settle it. Let's go."

" Go ? " Helen said. " But the garden ! Don't you want to wait ? "

" They won't find anything," he answered. " There's nothing there to find." He started towards the door. " Are you coming ? "

He did not wait, but strode out of the house.

Though Helen and Martin followed him at once, he was soon several yards ahead of them, giving no sign that he knew they were there, and it was not until he reached the doorway of the Swan that he paused, looking absently over his shoulder.

He seemed to be quite absorbed in his thoughts, and bleak thoughts they must have been to bring to his face the look that Helen saw there.

Inside, they found Myra and Hovard alone in the bar. On most evenings, at that hour, the bar would have been full, but the news of what was happening in the garden of Shipley's End had emptied the place like magic.

When Helen, Dreydel and Martin came in, Myra and

Hovard were engaged in a low-voiced quarrel. Both their faces were flushed and Myra, sitting bolt upright, was making fierce stabs at the air around her with an unlit cigarette. She was speaking rapidly but almost without moving her lips, which gave her face a frightening mask-like appearance. But when Helen saw Hovard's eyes, she thought that of the two he was in fact in the more dangerous mood.

He was aware before Myra that they were no longer alone and tried to check her flow of speech with a peremptory gesture. She took no notice of it and when she realised that she had an audience, merely raised her voice a little.

"No, no," she said venomously, "that was too much to expect. Too much indeed! I may have been an infatuated fool, I may have let that make me commit every idiocy imaginable, but for you to convince yourself that I might still be thinking of marrying you after you made it so clear last night that without a house and the money I can't lay my hands on I have no farther attractions for you, is an even worse idiocy than any of mine."

"Myra, for God's sake!" Hovard said. The tone was propitiatory but his eyes were still furious. "At least save it up till we're by ourselves, can't you?"

"Why should I?" she asked. "Martin is quite interested in my plans. Helen, no doubt, is curious about them also. And I'm quite sure Mr. Dreydel, whose motives I still know nothing about, is intensely curious about everything that happens to any of us. So I am supplying them with the information——"

She was interrupted by Hovard lumbering to his feet and making straight for the door.

Dreydel caught him by the arm and swung him back. "Just a moment. Let's hear what Mrs. Andras has to say, shall we?"

"She's got nothing to say," Hovard said. "She's just blowing off a lot of spite because of something I said to her last night, something I said as a joke."

"A joke!" Myra said. "Did you mean it as a joke

178

when you said that if Miss Gamlen—I mean, Mrs. Colliver—kept up her disappearing tricks, we'd never be able to get married ? Didn't you make it quite clear that unless I had the money there'd be no marriage ? It was after Helen had been to see me and told me about her aunt's having vanished from the house in Barnet. You said then——"

Hovard interrupted her again, this time by a fit of sneezing. In the midst of it, he muttered, " Damn you, damn you ! " several times, but it seemed to be to Dreydel that he was saying it, or perhaps even to the black kitten that Dreydel was carrying, not to Myra.

She went on, " And even if it was a joke, it showed me what you've been thinking all this time. You thought I was soon going to be a quite rich woman. Well, perhaps I am. But hasn't it occurred to you that if that were to happen, I might not be so anxious to marry you, that I might not find the idea of a man to keep me quite so attractive ? A rich widow can have quite a good time just being a rich widow. But for your information, may I make it perfectly clear now that, rich or poor, I have no intention of marrying you ? "

" May I congratulate you on the decision, Mrs. Andras ? " Dreydel said.

This caught her by surprise. She turned her head and stared at him.

" After all," Dreydel went on, " marriage can be a rather lethal business. Husbands should be picked with great care. It's as well to make sure, for one thing, how many wives they've disposed of before they got around to you. It's even a good thing sometimes to make sure how they treat dumb animals—such as small black kittens. Here, Hovard——" Holding the little purring animal in one hand, he thrust it towards Hovard.

" Take that damned animal away from me ! " Hovard shouted, stepping backwards.

With a quick movement, Dreydel tossed the kitten aside into a chair. His face had gone white. Suddenly it was a face that Helen had never seen before, with a look on it that she was glad never to have seen on any face.

But, as he stepped closer to Hovard, his voice was still quiet.

"Allergic to cats, Hovard? They make you sneeze, they make your eyes run. And you take pills for it—antihistamine pills. Not one of your own quack remedies, but ordinary antihistamine pills, on a doctor's prescription."

"What if I do?" Hovard said blusteringly. "I don't see——"

"Because you took one there in that house in Barnet when you'd killed Mrs. Colliver," Dreydel said. "And you swallowed it down with some water you poured into a sherry glass. And you locked the kitten in the coal-shed. And you were the man in the garden here—here at Shipley's End a year ago when you first came trying to buy the house—the man the Goodermans saw, the man Evelyn recognised——"

Dreydel's voice had been changing. It had risen and a kind of sob had come into it.

"What did you do with her, Poplar?" he shouted as he hurled himself at Hovard.

XIX

THAT YEAR the first snow fell early. One afternoon, half-way through December, the dim London sky grew speckled with moving flakes, looking, as they drifted past the window, not white, but almost grey-brown, like the clouds that let them fall. Yet by the evening, under the street-lamps in quiet streets, where the snow that lay on the pavements was not trodden into slush before it could pile up, a crisp and shining whiteness covered the ground.

When Helen's visitor arrived at her flat, he was powdered with white from head to foot. Having rung her bell, he paused for a minute or two in the doorway, knocking the caked snow off his shoes against the edge of the step and brushing his coat with his hands. Because of this, Helen was out on the landing, waiting for him, peering down with a look of uncertainty into the shadows, before he reached the turn in the staircase.

When she saw who it was, her face grew bright.

" But I thought you'd gone," she said. " I thought you'd gone right away."

" I wouldn't have gone," Dreydel answered, " without saying good-bye."

He followed her into the flat. The curtains, drawn over the tall windows, shut out the view of window-panes half obscured by the snow. The room was warm, with the gas-fire hissing and glowing redly in the fireplace. There were some roses in a bowl on a table.

Helen touched these as she passed.

" I thought perhaps these were good-bye," she said.

He smiled, shaking his head.

" But I am going to-morrow," he said.

" Flying ? "

" Yes."

She did not speak for a moment, then she said, " It'll be nice and warm out there—after this, I suppose."

" Yes, it will."

" And you've done what you came to do."

This time he did not answer.

She went on, " Why did you vanish, as you did, as soon as—as soon as you knew that they'd found Evelyn's body in the cellar of Hovard's house ? "

" I needed to do some thinking," he said. " I thought that perhaps you did too."

" Yes, but there were so many things I wanted to ask you. Besides . . ." But she did not seem to know what else to say.

" Ask them now," he suggested.

" Oh, I worked out a lot of it for myself," she said. " For instance, that Hovard—Poplar—whatever his name was, had been in Burnstone at about the right time of year to have been seen there by Evelyn and her friends. I saw him myself put a michaelmas daisy into Myra's buttonhole, saying that there'd been michaelmas daisies in the same vase when he first saw her there in the bar. D'you remember when we were having dinner together, I told you a lot about the spring and the autumn in Burnstone? I kept feeling I was almost saying something important, and I think that was what it was. But the description of him—how can that be made to fit?"

"Evelyn described him as a smallish, rather plump man with a pasty face and dark hair," Dreydel said. "And an obvious charlatan. It was that that put me all wrong, because there was Colliver ready-made to fit the description and I didn't trouble to look anywhere else. That was a fearful mistake, because there was Hovard too, who was certainly a charlatan and who had dark eyebrows, even if his hair had gone white, who was thick-set and whose florid face could easily have been pasty if he hadn't been long out of gaol. Prison-pallor is what it's called, I believe. And if you think of those grey cotton gloves that Poplar wore, that's more like the trick of someone whose finger-prints have been recorded by the police and who knows he's got to keep his tracks covered from the start, rather than of someone like Colliver, who's been on the edge of getting into trouble a good many times but never actually been arrested."

"But Hovard wasn't a small man," Helen said. "He wasn't particularly tall—not as tall as you or Martin. But I'd never think of describing him as smallish."

"That's because you aren't very big yourself," Dreydel answered. "And you always saw him with Mrs. Andras, who's unusually small and in a very perfectly proportioned way, so that Hovard always looked a great, clumsy, bearish figure beside her. But Evelyn was unusually tall. When I showed you her photograph, you pointed out that she was almost as tall as I was. So she'd naturally think of Hovard as smallish. He probably was at least two inches shorter than she."

"And you thought all this out," Helen said, "while you were driving to London in Martin's car."

"Most of it, though there were things in that house in Barnet that had been worrying me ever since I'd seen them. I'd no doubt when we were there that Colliver had done the murder and those fake spirit messages at first seemed only to confirm that. But later I began to wonder how he could have been so stupid as to leave them behind. And leaving her handbag, her writing-case and that slipper. . . . Her death was no use to him unless she disappeared and unless her disappearance could be made to look like all her other disappearances. That was what he and his sister had been working for patiently for the last year. They'd coaxed and frightened the poor woman into behaving so crazily that at last people would stop bothering to ask where she was. Possibly they didn't really want to do it, but when they found out that she was in any case dying, they hatched out the scheme in an attempt to keep hold of her property for a time. Colliver had already been forging her cheques for some time and that would quietly have gone on. Incidentally, when the police catch up with him, that may be the only offence they can hold him on. I doubt if he could be charged with intent to commit a murder that had already been committed by somebody else."

"Perhaps he didn't intend to murder her," Helen said.

"You mean that he was willing to wait until she died naturally and only then make her disappear?" Dreydel said. "I doubt it. I think taking that suburban house for her, where there'd be no landlady to watch what he did, and the big trunk there in the house, and his getting the garden dug so that a little extra digging wouldn't attract attention, meant that he'd come to the time when he was ready to do murder. After all, if he'd waited for her to die in her own time, it might have happened in some public place, or she might have been able to call help even into that terrible little lonely house, so that all his careful planning would have been wasted. But he was an almost pathetically blundering plotter. Everything he did was so suspicious that if he had got as far as the murder, he'd have been arrested at once. All the same, I didn't really think that he'd blunder to the extent that he apparently had in that house. And then it became fairly clear that your aunt's body had not been removed by him, but by Martin Andras. And that meant that whoever had done the murder had not minded if her body were found, or even wanted it to be found. And that suggested Mrs. Andras or Hovard. It was in the interests of both of them that Mrs. Colliver should stop her mysterious disappearances and turn up undeniably dead as soon as possible."

" So you suspected Myra too. I thought you did."

He shrugged his shoulders. " Her son did, didn't he ? Wasn't that why he did what he did ? He'd told her where Mrs. Colliver was, I suppose to discourage her marrying Hovard in a fit of optimism about her possible death. Then he found Mrs. Colliver murdered and he thought that even if his mother hadn't murdered her, she'd at least connived at it."

" Yes," Helen said. " He telephoned her. He told her not to tell anyone that she knew where Aunt Violet was."

"And she told us about that," Dreydel said, " just after Hovard had suddenly left the bar with some improbable excuse about wanting to telephone his lawyer. And he did that as soon as I took the kitten out of the box. He'd had one attack of trouble from contact with that kitten in the house in Barten and he'd cured it with his antihistamine pills. In the circumstances, he naturally didn't want to draw attention to his idiosyncrasy by asking us to remove the kitten, or by waiting around until his catarrh came back. It did come back, however, and he tried to pass it off as a cold, while Mrs. Andras mocked him because his own cold-cure wasn't any good."

" So that was why he locked the kitten in the coal-shed."

" Yes—except that I believe the person who actually did that was Mrs. Colliver herself. Think it out. If Hovard himself had wanted to get rid of the kitten, all he had to do was drive it out of the house. But the kitten had been put in the coal-shed, the key turned on it and the key brought back into the house. So I think that what happened was this. Hovard came to visit Mrs. Colliver. She thought it was an ordinary visit, offered him a drink and went out to the kitchen to get it. When she came back, the kitten followed her in. He asked her at once to remove it, possibly to take it right out of the house. But she'd have been afraid that a kitten as young as that, put out into the darkness, might easily have got lost. So, because there was nowhere else to put it safely, she put it in the coal-shed, automatically locking it, as she always did, and returning the key to the nail where it always hung. She expected, of course, to leave the kitten there only for half an hour or so. While she was outside, doing that, Hovard got out his pills, picked up a glass from the tray, went out to the kitchen and filled the glass with water, swallowed the pill and came back. When Mrs. Colliver returned, she thought he'd helped himself to gin, so she simply helped herself to some sherry, sat down by the fire again and drank it. And then Hovard killed her."

"And Mignon's Mad Tea Party for the cats—it was that that finally convinced you of all this," Helen said.

"I suppose so," he said. "The Collivers were cold-bloodedly cruel to your poor aunt, but no Colliver would be cruel to a cat without desperate necessity. And there was no necessity for anyone but Hovard to get rid of that kitten."

"But when Mignon fainted away when she saw that message you forged, what did you think? Do you believe what she told me, that she thought at long last she'd really been in communication with a spirit?"

"Why not?" he said. "Most fakes half-believe in themselves. That's what keeps them going. It must have been a perfectly terrifying experience for her, though by now, I imagine, she's worked out what really happened. Any more questions?"

"I don't think so." Turning away from him, she looked down at the red-hot rectangle of the fire. "You know, when you turned on Hovard, I thought you were going to kill him."

"I nearly did," he said.

"Yet d'you know what my clearest memory of that moment is? It's of Bertie's face at the door. It was white and twitching with terror and yet he was in heaven. Of course he's having a wonderful time now, with all the publicity."

Dreydel smiled. " I've got one question I want to ask."

" Go on, then."

" Where's Andras now ? "

" In Italy, I think, with Myra. She had a kind of breakdown, so he took her away. The police seem to think it was he who took the trunk back, so they let him off with a caution, and that's all. They seem to think he suspected that Hovard had already murdered several women and so was to be forgiven for having tried to protect his mother. Someone . . ." She looked up at him again. " Someone seems to have suggested to them that explanation of what happened."

" And you ? " he said. " You and Andras ? "

" I thought there was to be only one question."

" This is really part of the same one, isn't it ? "

" But you've known the answer to that all along," she said. " Martin isn't for me. He never has been."

" But you want him still, though you're afraid of what that might mean, and you won't fight for him."

She shook her head. " He'd never have done for me what he did for Myra, and really I'm thankful for that. That's what it all means. I would fight for him if I wanted him."

There was a silence. Then Dreydel said, " Helen, I'm going away to-morrow and after a little while I'm going to write to you. Will you answer my letter and will you answer it soon ? " He smiled wryly. " Remember I'm liable to get nervous if a letter isn't answered."

THE END

www.ingramcontent.com/pod-product-compliance
Ingram Content Group UK Ltd.
Pitfield, Milton Keynes, MK11 3LW, UK
UKHW022313280225
455674UK00004B/288